PRAISE FOR WILLIAM HAZELGROVE AND *THE PITCHER*

A Junior Library Guild Selection

Nominated for the *Printz Award* for Literary Excellence in Young Adult Fiction.

"Like all good baseball novels, Hazelgrove's *The Pitcher* has spit and dirt and leather and battles between boys. And like all good baseball novels, *The Pitcher* is also about more than just baseball. There are dreams here, and hope (and a mom, something even the best baseball novels often forget about). *The Pitcher* is a story about making lives, and in Hazelgrove's hands you can feel them taking shape."
—Billy Lombardo, Author of *The Man with Two Arms*

"Hazelgrove captures the essence of heartbreak and tragedy beautifully."
—The Denver Post

"Hazelgrove writes with warmth and feeling, his characters richly drawn, moving and evocative of its time."
—Booklist

"American Fiction is not dead ... Hazelgrove has skillfully revived it."
—*Library Journal*

"Hazelgrove has a natural grace as a storyteller that is matched by his compassion for his characters."
—*Chicago Sun-Times*

"Proof that despite the fleeting nature of trends, good writing survives. For this reason William Hazelgrove has more than survived."
—*Time Out Chicago*

The Pitcher
by William Hazelgrove

ISBN 9781938467592

Published by

an imprint of Morgan James Publishing

5 Penn Plaza, 23rd floor
c/o Morgan James Publishing
New York, NY 10001
212-574-7939
www.koehlerbooks.com

Publisher
John Köehler

Executive Editor
Joe Coccaro

In an effort to support local communities, raise awareness and funds, Morgan James Publishing donates a percentage of all book sales for the life of each book to Habitat for Humanity Peninsula and Greater Williamsburg.

Get involved today, visit www.MorganJamesBuilds.com

Also by William Hazelgrove

Ripples
Tobacco Sticks
Mica Highways
Rocket Man

Coming in Fall 2014
Real Santa

For Kitty, Clay, Callie,
and Careen

THE PITCHER

WILLIAM HAZELGROVE

NEW YORK
VIRGINIA

World Series Game Seven
1978 Baltimore Orioles versus St. Louis Cardinals
Busch Stadium, St. Louis
CBS Radio

...four to one in the ninth, Orioles. Langford is on the plate. He has been pitching for three games and has to be tired. Two outs. He winds up and there's the pitch to McGee. It's a foul tip and straight up and Orioles catcher Fiero flings his mask and it's caught! The Baltimore Orioles have just won the World Series! Jack Langford has pitched three games and allowed only five runs and has just won the World Series and there he goes jumping into the arms of catcher Fiero! What a game, folks! The only pitcher to win three complete games in a single World Series ... he will certainly be the MVP for the World Series ...outdueling Bob Mariano in this dramatic show of strength for this southpaw from South Dakota who hit a home run in game five and gave the Orioles the edge they needed ... unbelievable ... just unbelievable ... he will surely be the MVP for the World Series ...

Play Ball

The only thing that could stop me was myself.

—Jim Abbott

1

I NEVER KNEW I HAD AN ARM until this guy calls out, "Hey you want to try and get a ball in the hole, sonny?" I am only nine, but Mom says, "Come on, let's play." This carnival guy with no teeth and a fuming cigarette hands me five blue rubber balls and says if I throw three in the hole, we win a prize. He's grinning, because he's taken Mom's five bucks and figures a sucker is born every minute. This really gets me, because we didn't have any money after Fernando took off, and he only comes back to beat up Mom and steal our money. So I really want to get Mom back something, you know, for her five bucks.

I take the first rubber ball and throw it over my head and wham! The carnival guy looks at me and laughs. "Whoa! A ringer. Let's see you do it again, sonny." It's like something happens when I throw a ball. My arm windmills over the top then snaps down like a rubber band. It's like I'm following my arm. So I throw the second ball and he mutters, "Alright, let's see you get the next ball in." I mean we're Mexicans, and I think this guy figures he'll put one over on us.

I throw the next two balls and they go wild. I hit the top of the wood circle with one and the other one flies completely over the game. The carnival guy is grinning again because he knows I have only one more ball. I wind up like I had seen pitchers on television and *wham*, right in the hole again. He hands Mom a big white polar bear and takes the cigarette from his mouth.

"That looked like a sixty-mile-an-hour pitch to me," he says.

"I don't know," I reply, shrugging.

He nods and picks up the rubber balls.

"You should pitch, buddy," he says with one eye closed. "You have a hell of an arm."

I feel good about that, but I have never known a pitcher, except for the guy across the street who lives in his garage. When my friends come over, we lie on his driveway listening to ball-games like the ocean in the dark. Sometimes we listen to the Cubs when my man Zambrano is on the mound. It is cool lying on his drive in the Florida night listening to the game, because this dude pitched in a World Series. He beat Bob Mariano in the '78 Series. You can check it out on YouTube.

Joey, my best friend, likes to throw stuff under the garage to prod his dog to come out. The Pitcher has this chocolate Labrador, Shortstop, who sleeps on his driveway. That's the thing—he never opens the garage door all the way, just enough for the dog to slip under. You can see his white ankles and hear the game, but you never see the rest of him. We throw all sorts of stuff under his garage: rocks, sticks, oranges. Sometimes we sneak up and roll an egg under there. Shortstop eats the eggs and oranges, which really kills us. Joey and I figure the Pitcher is a drunk because his garbage can is full of this beer called Good Times. Dude ... who sits in a garage and drinks beer called *Good Times?*

Anyway, we usually end up playing ball in front of his house.

Joey says I have the fastest arm he's ever seen and that makes me feel good. I'm not so good at other things, like school, because I cannot focus and I give the teachers hell. Everything buzzes right over my head. Mom says I'm ... well I don't like to say it because it bothers the hell out of me. Let's just say reading is hard for me because the words jump around. So we go to these teacher conferences where Mom loses it. She's half-Puerto Rican and charges in there in her Target uniform and wants to know *why the hell isn't anybody helping my son.*

So when I found out I have an arm, I was like, wow, I'm good at something. A man at the police station timed me with a radar gun and all the cops crowded around. They had me throw a baseball five times and just shook their heads. That guy at the carnival was wrong about pitching sixty miles an hour, because the little numbers flashed 74 and 77. So after the cops timed me, we scraped up the money to join a team. I got a uniform with a couple different jerseys. A lot of people send their kids to camps and these baseball clinics and are on travel teams—but not us. We ended up in our neighborhood when Fernando was working and now Mom says we're just hanging on.

"Come on, bring it, Hernandez!" Joey shouts down the street.

He squats down in front of the Pitcher's house and beats his mitt. I bring the heat and sometimes I hit his glove but it's like I have this rocket with no guidance. When I draw back, this wild beast zings the ball through the air at seventy plus. The thing is, I don't have a change-up. A good change-up comes like a fastball but is about fifteen miles slower. With me it's all about heat. I only know one way to throw and sometimes Joey grabs it, but most of the time he chases it down the street. Here's my play. If I keep throwing in the street, maybe the Pitcher will come out. You know, just tell me how you control a pitch, because, really, I have no idea.

So one day I'm batting the ball in the street with Joey. It's one of those super-hot days in Florida where you just want to hide in the air-conditioning all day. The street is so hot we can feel it through our tennis shoes. I smack a low grounder to him that hits a station wagon, then shoots past Shortstop and under the Pitcher's garage. That's what we call him, the Pitcher, because that's what Joey's dad called him when he told us he won the Series. Joey's dad said he thought he was in his late fifties. I guess that's pretty old, because Mom is in her thirties and that seems old.

"That ball is gone, bro," Joey says, shaking his head.

I stare at the dark opening and can hear a ballgame.

"I'm getting it," I tell him, walking toward the garage.

"You're crazy man!" he shouts. "He's going to go psycho on you."

Yeah, I'm scared, but it's our last baseball. So I'm almost to the garage and my heart is bamming away in my chest when the door starts clanking up. Joey bolts across the street and I'm thinking about running too when I see the ball in the middle of the cement floor. It's just sitting there like a snowball in the dark. I'm staring now because there's a bed, a refrigerator, a desk, a lamp, and a television with a game on real low. Cans of Skoal go around the a La-Z-Boy like green buoys next to a stack of Good Times beer. There's even a microwave with beans and spaghetti on a board over a slop sink.

"What the f---," Joey says, coming back across the street.

Mom says I can't use the F-bomb, so I have to abbreviate. Anyway, like I said, none of us had ever seen the Pitcher before, but we didn't think he had his bed in the garage. We assumed he just hung out there to watch his games.

"I ain't going in there," Joey says, shaking his head.

He looks at me with his big dark Mexican eyes and shaved head. We had both shaved our heads against the heat and in our white T-shirts we look like brothers. Except Joey is older than me; everybody is older than me. I turn fourteen in September. Mom always said she should have held me back. I don't know, man; I would have felt pretty stupid in seventh grade instead of cruising toward high school.

I stare at the baseball just sitting there and I can feel the cooler air of the garage. Like I said, we didn't have another one.

"Yeah ... I'm getting it," I mutter, taking a step toward the garage.

Joey's eyes turn into fireballs.

"You go in there and that dude is going to grab your ass!"

Maybe the Pitcher is setting a trap, but I want our baseball. So I walk in. There's some old ratty fan whirring in the corner. The garage smells like dirty socks and cigarettes. The television murmurs ...*full count. Baltimore ahead by three* ... I turn back to Joey in a patch of sun. He looks like he's a million miles away.

"Grab the ball and run, bro. Get out of there, man!" he shouts.

I walk farther into the garage with my heart slamming against my chest. Cigarettes are stubbed in cans, on paper plates, even on the floor. The Skoal cans are everywhere. I reach our baseball and take another step, then stop and stare at these pictures. The Pitcher is on the mound in his windup. Then he has a bat over his shoulder like one of those All-American guys on baseball cards. Then the dugout pictures with one leg up, standing with other ballplayers. I just stare at these faded pictures tacked up in the garage while the baseball game plays. Some of the pictures are black-and-white and some are color, and this is my dream, you know. I want to make the high school baseball team in the fall and one day, I want to pitch for the Chicago Cubs in Wrigley Field.

We used to live in Chicago and Mom says you can do anything if you believe it enough. I believe I can make the high school team, although only thirty guys make the freshman team out of one hundred. League ball ends after eighth grade, so you got to make it or you just disappear. Guys have been training for years to make the team, with lessons, travel teams, camps, and personal trainers. Everyone knows high school ball is the cutoff.

You don't make the high school team, then it's game over.

I keep walking along the garage wall between the rakes, brooms, and shovels, and I can't take my eyes off the pictures. The Pitcher is looking sideways, one leg up, his body pivoted, with the ball cocked back. I wonder if he feels the way writers and painters talk sometimes—like the way I do, like you aren't even there. That's how I feel when I pitch; it's like I wake up when I hear the ball smack the catcher's mitt.

"Get the ball!" Joey calls again, taking another step toward the street.

I turn back to the wall and stare at this one black-and-white picture. The Pitcher is jumping into the arms of his catcher with his legs up. The catcher has his mask off and he has his mouth open and the Pitcher is yelling to the sky. He just won the World Series against the Cardinals. The World Series. I lean close, hearing the fan, the ballgame, the heat, trying to feel what he was feeling as he jumped into his catcher's arms.

"C'mon, Hernandez!"

I leave the wall and step over the Skoal and walk past the pyramid of Good Times cans and pick up our baseball. Then I turn and walk real fast out into the sunshine. And that's when the garage door starts rolling down. Joey bolts and runs down the street and I whip around, thinking the Pitcher is behind me, with my heart bam bam bamming. The door drops, then goes back up a third, and then just stops. And the dog, he just groans and rolls over like nothing ever happened. And the ballgame gets turned back up like it never stopped.

2

WE ARE PLAYING TRI CITY and Coach Gino doesn't like to lose. He's a dark Puerto Rican and wears aviators with his hat low and talks a million miles a minute. *¿Qué Pasa? What's happening? ¿Qué Pasa?* Everybody wants to be on Tri City, but we ended up on the Marauders with a five hundred average. The problem is John Gallo can't get a pitch to the plate and Gino is giving everyone the take sign. I'm crunching sunflower seeds when I hear Mom talking to Coach Devin.

"Get him out of there, Devin!"

Coach Devin is Eric's dad. Eric always pitches first and he is our number three batter. Devin never balls him out for dropping flies or missing grounders. But the truth is Eric doesn't miss grounders or pop flies and he's probably the best hitter I've ever seen. But he's always stealing sunflower seeds or somebody's hat and knows he's the best. He's part of Team Payne, which is what his family calls themselves. His mom drives a van with *Tempayn* on the plates. He's also the guy who got me suspended from Napoleon Junior High.

It started in the lunchroom the first day of school. Eric swooped up my dessert and gestured to his homeboys. "Gonna have me some beano cupcake!" Yeah that's what he said. So picture this: one of those Hostess cupcakes with the swirly drizzle across the top and the chocolate slightly hardened with the stub of cream inside. I love those, man, and now picture my cupcake dangling above the Crest-brushed teeth of one Eric Payne. And this same dude is saying over and over: *"I'm going to have me some beano cupcake!"*

Beano cupcake—beano cupcakes maybe, but not *beano cupcake*. So I grab up this plastic knife and all his homeboys start shouting, *"The beano has a knife! The wetback has a knife! Watch out, man, he is one of those psycho dudes!"* And that's when Mr. Truss, the PE teacher, karate chops my wrist as everyone pulls back like I'm the big bad gangbanger. There aren't many Mexicans in our school and I've had a few run-ins with teachers before.

"I want to know what you are doing to those boys who called my son a wetback and a beano!"

That's what Mom said at the team meeting. Dr. Freedom, the dean of Napoleon Junior High, sat up straight. She wore this blue suit with a silver bird and old lady granny glasses with a ton of makeup. She stared at Mom and me like we just came across the border.

"We have zero tolerance for violence in this school, Ms. Hernandez," she said in this calm teacher voice.

"It was a plastic knife!"

Which was my point. Mom asked her again what she was going to do about the boys hitting me with a racial slur. "We have no evidence anyone called your son a wetback or a beano," Dr. Freedom continued, touching up her glasses. "But we have zero tolerance for any type of violence."

"So you just punish the Mexican defending himself," Mom shot back.

Dr. Freedom rolled her hands. Napoleon Junior High is a

Blue Ribbon school and they don't want some Mexican kid to screw up their national average. If you aren't like in a wheelchair or something, they think you are just lazy. So they hope I'll just kick it in, but my grades have really tanked, because when I'm in class, I'm really not there. It's the same way on the mound. I just float off sometimes and Mom knows that.

Even before the cupcake deal, Eric had it in for me. It really started at the tryouts. When I pitched I hit the backstop, but there was a coach from The Flyers there. After I was done he walked up to me and said, "You got the fastest damn arm I have ever seen on a kid your age. That's a God-given gift." Eric was next to me and turned red, then threw his mitt on the ground and kicked his batting helmet across the dugout. Ever since then, it's been war between us.

"Pull him, Devin!"

That's Mom again. Devin has a goatee, wraparound sunglasses, chewing gum. Supposedly he played college ball and pitched. He looks at his assistant coach in her blue and red coach's jersey tucked into black athletic shorts. Mom's curly hair flows over the back of the jersey in a long ponytail. Devin squints toward the field as John throws and *crack!* The batter blasts it down first base and it stays fair. Tri City rotates in two runs and we are chasing two. Devin kicks the dirt and swears. He pushes back his hat, pinching his chin worriedly.

"Even if Ricky is a little wild they are going to go after it," Mom continues, gesturing to the field.

I know if Devin was left alone he would never play me. I don't have a lot of control, but how can I get better if I never play? His entire approach to coaching could be summed up in one sentence, *We are getting the boys ready to play high school ball.* He doesn't steal home and rarely steals second if he thinks the catcher can throw down. He goes for the out almost every time and lets the runners score.

Devin takes this long breath and turns to me on the bench.

"You ready to throw, Ricky?"

I jump up and nod. "Sure coach!"

"Need a warm-up?"

"Just a few from the mound," I say, catching Mom's wink.

Devin holds up his hand to the umpire.

"Time, Blue!"

"New pitcher! New pitcher!"

I love that sound when *I'm* the new pitcher, when I'm drilling them into Eric's mitt like there's no tomorrow. Mom calls it being in *the zone*. I come over the top and the ball arcs down and cuts the strike zone like a rocket through a tire. *Whoosh!* Other coaches shake their heads. I wouldn't want to bat against me when I'm on.

I take the ball from Eric and breathe in the cut grass, watching dust tornado around home plate. I can hear kids screaming on the playground behind the field. Blue pulls down his mask and points to me, "PLAY BALL!"

It's like sixty feet from the mound to the plate for the majors and for league play it's sixty feet. Mom is by the dugout sifting dirt through her fingers as Eric gives me a finger to the outside. I breathe and position my fingers on the ball. I breathe again, kick up my leg, lasso my arm over my head, whipping the ball down toward the batter. I hear the cannon pop from Eric's mitt.

"Strike!"

Marauder parents clap and people shake their heads.

"ALRIGHT, RICKY!" Mom calls out.

"JUST LIKE THAT, RICKY," Devin shouts from the dugout.

"CONCENTRATE ON THE BATTER," Mom calls again, squatting down.

Eric touches his thigh for an inside pitch. I breathe again and kick up my leg and let fly. POP! The umpire jabs a finger and screams again.

"Steeerike!"

The kid whiffed on that one. He's mad now and I know it. You want them mad so they will swing at a seventy-mile-an-hour pitch. A lot of kids won't swing at a fast pitch. They just freeze and their coach gives the take sign. The take sign is your enemy when you are unsure. I hear somebody say, "How fast is he throwing?"

"He's balking. Watch the balk, Blue."

That's Coach Gino. He is one of the best at knocking a pitcher off his game. I've got two strikes and the batter is crowding the plate to force a ball. I tug on my cap, dig my cleat against the rubber. All I have to do is give him another straight fastball. The batter holds out his bat and adjusts his helmet. He wants it now and taps his cleats against the plate, adjusts his wristband, moving the bat in a slow circle. I shake off Eric's signal, but he's the captain of our team and jabs his thigh again for an inside fastball.

He gives me the signal again. I breathe, kick back, and throw inside, but my arm doesn't track straight and my release is wrong. I hear a *thump* like someone kicking a pumpkin. Then everybody is running because the batter is on the ground holding his ribs with snot pumping out his nose. I feel like dying, because hitting somebody is the worst thing a pitcher can do.

There is only one incident I know where a guy was killed by a pitch. It happened in the twenties when this guy named Ray Chapman of the Cleveland Indians stepped into Carl May's inside fastball. The baseball cracked into Ray's temple and he went down with blood streaming out his ears and mouth. They say he had a three-inch crack in his skull.

"Breathe breathe ... you're OK. You're OK," Coach Gino says, helping the kid sit up. He's blotchy and gasping to get air into his lungs. His mother is going *"Oh, Oh, Oh"* with her hand over her mouth. My face is burning and I hear somebody say *Mexican,* and then something I don't want to hear. I stare at the ground and move dirt with my cleat. Eric comes up to me and shakes his head.

"I signaled a curve," he says loudly.

"No you didn't," I cry out and feel the world shift. I'm suddenly like *the Mexican* and he's the big American tourist. It's the cupcake thing all over again. He's the favored pitcher for the high school team and wants to make sure *nobody* shows him up, especially some Mexican kid with a fast arm.

Coach Gino looks up in his wraparound sunglasses mirroring the field.

"HEY COACH, YOUR BOY NEEDS TO CONTROL HIS PITCHES!" he shouts, making sure the umpire hears him.

Mom opens her mouth, her chin beginning to move.

"It was just a bad pitch," Devin replies, waving Mom off.

"He shouldn't be using all that heat if he can't control it," he continues, shaking his head like this was our plan or something. Gino helps the batter to his feet to a smattering of applause. A couple of Tri City players flip me off as I walk back to the mound. I feel like hiding in the dugout, man, but Mom knows what I'm thinking. She just nods to me.

"You shouldn't put someone out there who doesn't have control," Gino finishes up, saying it loud enough for everyone to hear.

"Yeah, yeah," Devin mutters, walking back to our side.

Everyone goes back to their dugouts and the parents settle into their chairs. "*Maybe he should slow his pitch down*" floats from the other side. I try and clear my mind. I take a breath and come out of the stretch, but I throw high and rattle the backstop. I do that three more times and Mom comes out with a time call. She walks up onto the mound and it's just the two of us.

"What's going on there , champ?" she asks, giving me a quick hand squeeze. She pulls her glasses up into her curly dark hair and looks tired.

Mom snaps her fingers in my face.

"Hey, earth to Ricky ... come in, Ricky" she says.

"Yeah ... sorry, Mom," I mumble.

She tugs on the brim of her hat and looks at me.

"Are you taking a breath between pitches?"

"Yeah."

She stares at me and I can see myself in her sunglasses. I can also see Eric with his mask off talking to Devin and the parents sitting in their lawn chairs. The umpire is glancing at his watch. "Look ..." Mom turns to me. "I know you feel bad about hitting that boy. You just have to shake it off and concentrate on Eric's mitt and getting the pitch in the strike zone. You can do this, Ricky," she says, keeping her eyes locked on mine.

"Yeah ... OK," I murmur.

She holds up her fist for a knuckle bump.

"You ready to knock them dead, Carlos?"

She always says that because Carlos Zambrano is my man. He burns them down, although he's been in a slump and got sent to the bullpen. But everyone knows it's just for show.

"Yeah, " I say, bumping her back.

"That's *coach* to you, pal. So, give this guy a fastball and let's get out of here."

I watch her leave and see Eric's Mom talking to her husband, Coach Devin. Ever since the cupcake deal, she looks at me like I'm a criminal. If you're Mexican, you know the look. She's tall and skinny with these bulging brown eyes that dare people to screw with her. To me, she looks like someone who doesn't eat enough. Anyway, I know what she's saying to Devin.

Pull him!

So I try and hit the zone, but I have lost control. I walk two more batters and Devin calls time and then I'm walking back to the dugout. Mrs. Payne watches me the whole way like I just pulled another knife. And not a plastic one either. Eric finishes up the side and comes into the dugout. He has these weird blue eyes and a blond crew. He grins at me and spits sunflower seeds on my shoe.

"You really suck, beano," he says, the way you would say good morning.

3

A FEW WEEKS LATER MOM and I are sitting on our porch after one of our games. She is smoking a cigarette, looking real pale. She's had lupus a long time and says it's like chicken pox; once you have it you have it. I've been hearing her puke lately and I know she hasn't gone to the doctor because we lost our health insurance.

She got fired from Target right before school let out. They cooked up something about her long lunches. Mom says it's because she passed around some petition against that Arizona immigration law. Mom says the law is un-American. She says any Mexican in Arizona who doesn't have papers can be sent back and they will do the same thing in Florida. Sitting on the porch is where we have our best talks. She's usually calmer there and explains stuff to me or just says what she's thinking. Like a friend, you know.

She lifts her arm and points across the street.

"He was a pitcher?"

"Yeah. MLB, Mom," I reply. "He even pitched in a World Series. Straight up. The dude is the real thing."

I just finished telling her about the baseball going under the Pitcher's garage and she's staring across the street. Devin had given this big speech at our last game about making the high school team and I think that got Mom thinking. She takes another drag of her cigarette .

"You need a coach," she says quietly.

She says it just like that, smoking her Marlboro with her foot bobbing. She knows that if I don't make the high school team then my posters of the Cubs and the Yankees, and photos of Giants speedballer Juan Marichal, triple Cy Young winner Pedro Martinez and my man Zambrano, won't mean anything. You got to start somewhere and that somewhere is high school ball. The tryouts are less than three months away in August. I'm so worried about making the team, I don't even feel good about having graduated from eighth grade.

The graduation ceremony was lame. I listened to some Kanye, Eminem, and this old Alice Cooper tune, *School's Out For Summer*, a tune I ripped from the Internet. Mom was in the bleachers in a red off-the-shoulder number with her hair pinned up. She waved and I heard her voice all the way across the gym.

"HEY RICKY! RICKY! RICKY!"

Jimmy nudged me in our folding chairs.

"Man, your Mom is kind of hot," he murmured.

I jammed my elbow in his side. "Dude, that's my Mom!"

"Sorry, man," he said, shrugging. "Just saying."

So then Mr. Simons motioned our row up. I got like nothing under that slippery robe and you could see my bare ankles and oversized Nikes. Rumors swirled I was going to do something, you know, like flip off Principal Bailey, punch out Dr. Freedom. I thought about doing a little Napoleon Dynamite dance on the way out, but I really didn't have the stomach for more drama. "Here you go, son. Congratulations," the man from District 505 said, shaking my hand, giving me my plastic diploma. I raised my hand and Principal Bailey opened his and that's when Mom shouted, "GO RICKY. YOU SHOWED THEM!"

People turned to the woman snapping pictures with her phone. Mom faced them all with her Latino attitude, daring the entire gymnasium to mess with her. Principal Bailey shook my hand and stared at Mom like he could scarcely believe what just happened.

"Congratulations, Ricky," he said. "Your mother ..." he trailed off.

"Yeah, I know," I said, nodding, grinning sheepishly.

And that was it.

Summer.

So Mom stares at the baseball on the porch a moment longer, then stubs her cigarette and jumps up. "C'mon. Time to practice," she commands, motioning to the street. I'm still in my uniform, but we go into the street and start throwing the ball. Lately Mom has been reading on the Internet about pitching and brings printouts with her sometimes. Even though she's my coach there's a lot she doesn't get about baseball. Like she has been reading about breathing lately and so every time before I pitch, I got to breathe. I never knew breathing had anything to do with pitching.

Mom starts throwing the ball and looking over at the garage. She's still in her Marauders jersey with her Oakleys as she wails the ball to me. My Mom has some heat, man. "Bring it to me, Carlos!" she shouts. Mom is hunched down and I go into my windup, but I don't bring the heat. I'm a little wild and if you have a seventy-five-mile-an-hour arm, man, you got to be careful. Mom stands up and frowns, gesturing to the sky.

"What the hell was that?"

"My fastball."

"There was nothing fast about that pitch, *cabrón*."

Mom beats her mitt again and squats down.

"Don't forget to take your breath and keep your shoulder square," she calls as I set myself again. And that's when I hear Fernando's Harley rumbling down the street. Mom turns and shakes her head. The courts told Fernando he was supposed to pay us, but when he gets hard up he comes and borrows money. I asked Mom once why she gives it to him. She just shrugged and said it was because he's my father. I quit thinking he was my father a long time ago.

Fernando parks his Harley, which is pretty sick. Chromed Super Glide. Mom still doesn't know where he got the money for it. She says its part of his midlife crisis, which I call his asshole crisis. Fernando walks up in his sleeveless T-shirt and shades like he's *Mr. Dad*. He gives me the knuckle bump and the gangbanger hug.

"Hey, bro, how's baseball?"

"Good," I mutter.

"Hey, man, we got to catch a Marlins game, you know, bro," he says, giving me another knuckle bump. He always says that and we never go and I always say, "Yeah, that's cool." It's like our ritual, you know. Maybe it makes him feel better to say it or something. He went Kanye somewhere and tattooed up with the gold chains and low rides his pants down to his knees. He looks pretty stupid, but I just smile.

"Throw it, man," he calls out with his shades low on his nose.

I toss the ball and he makes all these pitching motions like he's Zambrano. He tries to tell me about pushing off the rubber and hiding the ball in my mitt. I listen and smile while he acts like a major league pitcher. Then he looks at the garage with Shortstop asleep on the driveway. He squints, shaking his head real slowly.

"That dude still in there, huh?"

"Yeah."

"Man ..." Fernando strokes his goatee and shakes his head. "He's the real shit."

That is as close as Fernando comes to giving *anybody* a compliment. He turns to my mom and his voice gets low. I know what's next. I know his play.

"Oh come on, man ... you spend all this money on his f----- -- baseball," he says loudly, picking at her jersey. Mom whips around and faces him, her voice like ice water. "Go borrow it from your bimbos, Fernando," she tells him. Mom is like maybe five foot, but makes up for her height with her personality. She slaps off his hand because now he's trying to get all lovey-dovey. Mom points down the street and tells him in so many words to get the hell away from her. Most of the words I can't even use, man.

His dark pirate eyes come together and his tattoos swell.

"Yeah, man ... you spend all your time with him and what do I get?"

"What you deserved," Mom snaps, turning away.

"I come to you and you won't even give a man a boost of *fifty bucks!*"

Mom gets in his face with her chin moving and her eyes rocking.

"Why don't you sell that motorcycle you bought and can't afford?"

Fernando slaps her hand away like a pesky fly.

"Don't tell me what to do, bitch."

"I'm not givin' you any money, Fernando," Mom says, turning away.

Then he starts walking toward our house and she tries to grab him. That's when he turns and hits her in the jaw. *Smack!* Ain't like the movies, man. Fernando is like six-two and probably two-twenty. Mom goes down like a sack of clothes and blood churns red out of her mouth. My heart pounds away as I jump on his back and claw at his eyes.

"DON'T YOU HIT HER!"

It's like I'm not thinking, but this has happened before too.

We fly around in the street with Fernando screaming at me to get off of him. "Don't you hit her!" I yell again, pounding on his head. We twirl in the street like a circus act and I'm about to fall off when I hear glass shatter. Fernando stops and stares because his motorcycle windshield is in a million pieces. He throws me back and I hit the pavement like *bump bump*. He stares at the windshield in the street, then starts screaming, almost crying.

"What the hell! What the hell! *My bike man ... my f------ bike ....*"

I help Mom up from the ground. Her lip is bleeding and getting fat. She turns and spits a mouthful of blood at Fernando.

"Get out of here you f------ asshole before I call the cops!"

Fernando is looking around like somebody is hiding in a bush. He stops and stares at the Pitcher's garage for a long moment. He finally gets on the Harley and looks pretty funny, man, behind the few shards of glass. Mom goes inside to wash out her mouth and see if she needs a stitch in her front lip. I stand there breathing hard and watching Fernando rumble down the street. I pray somebody will hit him. Like I'm not talking about a car hitting him, man, I'm talking like a semi with a load of F10 pick-up trucks, so all that will be left of Fernando is a big splotch on the street. Then the firemen or whoever can just wash his sorry ass away.

4

MOM AND I ARE STARING at this old baseball I found in the bushes next to Fernando's bike. It's like a comet or something from outer space because it's from another world. The baseball is almost the color of mud with painted grass stains and heavy like it's waterlogged. The stitching has started to unravel on one side and is no longer red, but the color of old blood. Mom puts her cigarette in her mouth and turns the ball around on the kitchen table like it's got something written on it. She ashes her Marlboro and looks at me.

"You think he threw it?"

"It wasn't there before and something shattered the windshield," I point out, shrugging.

Mom keeps turning the ball. It's like she is seeing something in that baseball, because next thing I know she grabs the ball and says, "Come on." We cross the tar-warmed street and hit the Pitcher's yard overgrown with whatever grows in Florida. Shortstop looks up as we go on the porch that looks like nobody walked on it for like a million years. Mom smooths her hair back, then rings the doorbell, staring at the baseball like it's her passport. I'm kind of nervous because of all the stuff Jimmy and I have thrown under his garage door.

Mom waits, standing up real straight, then rings the doorbell again. I look at our bungalow with the stucco peeling off that Fernando said he was going to fix. The same way he said he was going to coach me. I remember he used to get this funny look when I pitched and the ball popped his mitt. Mom said he was jealous because I have something God gave me and God didn't give Fernando shit. I'm down with God by the way. You got to be, man, when you're Mexican and poor.

"I think he's in the garage, Mom," I say after she rings the doorbell three more times.

Mom does it by the book. Like putting on her blinkers when nobody is around or looking both ways when there are no cars anywhere. She says you got to have good habits and that's why she always is on me about my homework.

So now we are walking toward the garage and I'm really nervous.

"Mom ... what are you doing?" I whisper, but she just keeps walking in her jersey with the blood on the collar and her hat pulled low. I really think we should just go back to the house. Jimmy says the Pitcher has a shotgun and has taken a shot at Juan down the street for throwing dog crap under his garage. So I'm not down with Mom whamming on his garage door, *which she is doing right now!*

"Mr. Langford!"

I can see the paint has flaked off of in these big patches. Shortstop is staring at us. I hear the crowd of a ballgame and then it stops. Now my heart is really pounding and I have that funny feeling like right before I pitch. We hear shoes scuffing the cement like something out of a horror movie. The tips of these old brown shoes appear under the garage, like the kind of shoes dudes in suits wear. I can smell his cigarette.

"He's right there, Mom," I whisper. *"What are you doing?"*

"I'm giving him back his baseball," she whispers.

"It might not even be his!"

Mom looks at me. "I thought you said it was his."

"I said I thought it *might* be his—"

She rolls her shoulders.

"Then I'll just ask him ... *Mr. Langford?"*

Mom is frowning now because he's right there. She doesn't put up with weirdness from anyone. When Jimmy comes over with his hat backward and his pants low riding, she tells him to put that hat right and pull up his pants. That's because she was real poor, even poorer than we are now. She says if you act like you are poor, then you *are* poor.

"Mr. Langford!"

"Mom, let's just go," I whisper. "Forget about the baseball!"

I'm making a motion to Mom like, *let's get out of here.* Because it's like there is a ghost or something just inches away from us. I point to his shoes and Mom clears her throat and speaks in a calmer voice.

"Mr. Langford, I have your baseball. I want to talk to you," she says to the door.

The shoes move slightly and scuff the cement. Then we hear something smack the floor and I see brown juice spatter the cement. He clears his throat, this low gravelly voice coming through the wood door.

"Yeah ... so talk."

"I have your baseball, Mr. Langford. But I want to ask you a question," Mom continues, leaning close to the peeling garage.

"It's your nickel."

Mom kicks her hip out and starts moving her chin. "Well most people talk face-to-face. How about you lift this garage and I can give you your baseball and we can have a conversation?"

I see the tips of his shoes move again.

"Keep the baseball," he mutters, his shoes scuffing away.

Mom pounds the garage and the whole thing shakes. I figured he would come out and kill us or something. Mom holds her brow like she has a terrific headache.

"Let's leave, Mom," I whisper again, motioning to our house.

She shakes her head and stares at the garage.

"It's rude to keep a garage down, Mr. Langford, when someone wants to thank you!"

We wait and I can hear the wind in the trees. Shortstop groans and Mom is standing there with the baseball, her head down again. I just don't see this dude talking to us. I see us turning around and walking back to our house. Then Mom just starts talking anyway.

"I need a coach for my son, Mr. Langford," she begins again. "My son has a gift, but he needs a pitching coach ... someone who can teach him control and develop his arm. The high school baseball tryouts are coming up and he doesn't have a change-up." Mom pauses and holds her head high. "I will pay you one hundred dollars a week to coach my son, Mr. Langford!"

One hundred bucks a week! I know we don't have that, but once Mom sets her head to something, she finds a way. Just like when we started selling chocolate bars so I could play league ball. We stood outside the Jewel and some people just gave us the Mexican Death Stare like we were stealing their wallet. But a lot of people bought the bars and we sold more than anyone else on the team.

Mom and I wait for what seems like an hour, then the Pitcher's shoes scuff the cement again.

"I ain't no coach."

"I will pay you," Mom says again.

"I ain't nobody's coach," he says like someone putting up a wall.

Mom puts her head down, holding the ball like a Bible.

"My son has a great arm ... a gift, Mr. Langford. I will pay you—"

"I don't want your goddamn Mexican money."

Mom grits her teeth and her eyes start moving back and forth. She opens her mouth just as his scratchy voice comes through the garage, "... tell him to take a finger off his fastball and it'll go ten miles slower." That knocks Mom off, because a pearl has just rolled out from under the garage. We look at each other like we have just hit the lotto. Because here is the thing; if the Pitcher gives us one pearl, he might give us another.

His shoes then scuff away and we hear the ballgame come back on. Mom leans close to the garage.

"Mr. Langford?"

The television gets louder and I know he is gone.

"Let's go, Mom," I murmur, taking a step toward our house.

She looks at me, then the old baseball she's still holding. Mom hesitates, then leans down and rolls the baseball under the garage like a thank you card.

5

FERNANDO COMES TO MY NEXT game drunked up and hollering by the fence.

"Watch that dude, Ricky! He's coming home!"

Devin is giving him daggers and Mom is frowning, because Fernando is behind the dugout with his tattoos and greased hair and he's hanging on the fence. He's calling the umpire an idiot and a blind dumbass. And you can see the umpire is thinking about kicking him out of the park. It's happened before.

I'm catching and we are neck and neck with this Thunder team. I have a runner on third who is off base and dancing around. I'm trying to do two things at once. Eric's slider is off and his curve isn't breaking and his fastball has lost its gas. He's loaded the bases and complaining I'm not holding my mitt in the right spot. He isn't even close to hitting the spots, but he's not going to get pulled either. That's the way it is, man, when your dad is the coach.

Devin never really wanted an assistant coach. Mom just

started coming to practices. He didn't even give her a jersey for the first few games. She gets all over him when he plays favorites. Like Lance at short who has no baseball sense at all. *Nada.* But Lance's dad comes to every game and sits behind the plate in one of those folding chairs with the shade guard and plows through two bags of peanuts and hollers at Lance. "Chew leather, buddy! Chew leather!" Toby Yostremski's dad gets really pissed, because when Lance went off to Bible camp, we won three games in a row. Then Lance came back and Toby went out to right field again.

Fernando keeps laying it on.

"Oh man, these guys can't hit. They are getting the take sign, man. They are afraid of you guys!"

The coach on the third baseline glances toward him. They got two away and we are in the sixth. Eric is holding this guy at two and two. He always asks for me to catch for him because I can throw down on second and pass balls don't exist.

"Oh, bro ... that was no ball. C'mon, Blue, what the hell!"

That's Fernando again.

I breathe the dust and pound my mitt, which makes more dust. The batter is rolling his hands figuring he can get hold of Eric's fastball. The umpire hunches and brings up his chest protector. Eric has a change-up, a curve, a slider, a sinker, but no heat on his fastball. It's like you either have heat or you don't, but Eric can control the ball, which is something, yours truly, cannot.

"Watch him, Ricky! Man, he's coming," Fernando blares out.

I glance down the baseline and the runner is almost halfway and hunched like he's on springs. I yell at Eric, who has his glove up, "Watch the delayed steal!" Most coaches won't go for delayed steals because they think it's cheap and most of the time it never works. You have to time your steal to the second the ball goes back to the pitcher. That's why Eric doesn't believe it's going to happen and shouts, "Just give me the fricking ball!"

I glance at the runner where the third base coach is squatting. I really don't want to give the ball to Eric. The third base coach has been sending his guys way down the baseline all game. You can just tell some guys like to send their kids and this dude is definitely one of them. Also the third base coach is a dad who doesn't know what he's doing. He's giving all these goofy signals and the kid isn't even looking at him. That's how I know he is going to try and steal home.

"Throw me the fricking ball, Hernandez!"

Fernando yells out just then.

"Watch that motherf----- on third!"

Now Mom is yelling.

"Watch him, Ricky! Watch him!"

And I have Eric glaring at me and the dude on third poised like a rocket. I really don't want to do it, but I throw the ball. Baseball is like that; sometimes you just do something even though you know better. The runner bolts just as I throw and everybody screams.

"He's coming! He's coming!"

Eric takes the ball and then turns away. I'm squatting down with my mitt up and I hear Fernando screaming above the rest.

"TAG THE MOTHERF-----, RICKY!"

And then Eric does something that even now I can't believe. He throws a blooper. The ball sails in like a slow-moving satellite as I hear the runner pounding toward me. I have to just wait there with my mitt up. His cleats are drumming closer and I'm trying to hurry that ball before the runner reaches me. The ball hits my glove as he smashes into my side. *Boom!* The air pops out of my lungs and I skid on the ground and taste the dust. Then I hear all this yelling and Mom is over me, her eyes worried.

"*Ricky! Ricky!* Just try and get your breath!"

That's the thing. I can't. I try and get some air into my lungs, but it's tough. The other coach and Devin are red-faced and nose-to-nose. Devin is shouting with his finger, doing one of those Lou Piniella numbers.

"He charged him! He charged him! He's supposed to slide!"

This fat guy with a goatee is screaming right back.

"He was blocking the plate! Blocking the plate!"

You're supposed to slide into home plate. It's considered dirty baseball to charge the catcher. Most dudes won't do it, but some people will do anything to win.

I stand up groggily and Mom is dusting me off. The Thunder coach just keeps shaking his head.

"He blocked the plate! He blocked the plate!"

Just then I see Fernando. He's running behind the backstop and bulls out of the dugout entrance like a locomotive. He crosses home plate and *tackles* the Thunder coach. I see the dude's clipboard fly through the air, then his glasses, then I see the coach fly through the air. He lands in the dust just like I did. Fernando stands up with his tattoos, sunglasses, and cutoff Harley shirt, holding his arms wide

"Yo sorry, man! You were blocking the f------ plate!"

And everybody just freaks. The umpire throws Fernando out and he tells the umpire he's going to kick his ass. Then Mom is yelling at him to get off the field. And the Thunder coach is groaning in the dirt while Fernando screams about somebody hitting his son. Which kills me, man, because you know, he hits his son all the time.

6

GRANDMA IS COOL. SHE USED to take care of me in Chicago and was always baking cookies and buying me whatever I wanted while Mom and Fernando worked. She moved to Arizona a while ago and I think that's why Mom is so buzzed out. I mean I can't follow all the news programs she watches with everybody freaking out and marching in the streets. Mom says it's something every American should be concerned about because if they take away one person's rights, then they can take away anybody's. I always look for Grandma in the demonstrations in Arizona, but I never see her.

Whenever she calls she starts chattering in Spanish. *"Grandma, English, English, No Española,"* I tell her, because I don't speak Spanish except for *buenos dias* and *nada* and all the corny words you hear on television. It's just not my language, but Grandma thinks it is. "Why not?" she asks every time she calls. "You should be able to speak Spanish *and* English!"

I was born in *Chicago*. Arizona is where Mom came in with

Grandma and Granddad. Mom left for Chicago to become a dancer like Paula Abdul. Straight up. She still has all her CDs. Mom's built like a dancer; all legs, short waisted, muscular, a long graceful neck. But if Mom had a dream it was to be Paula Abdul. I once asked her why it didn't happen and she said it just didn't, besides she had me, and that's a lot better than being Paula Abdul.

I don't know, man. I think I would trade me to get rid of Fernando and be Paula Abdul. He broke into the house the night after he bowled down the Thunder coach. Fernando just punched in the screen and unlocked the window. Mom says she would have called the cops except she doesn't want the father of her son in jail. I have to say, it wouldn't bother me.

"How is your mother's health?"

That's always Grandma's first question. She knows about Mom's lupus and says Mom doesn't take care of herself. I have to agree with her. A couple of times I have gone to use the toilet and it was full of blood. Not like a little blood, like crayon-colored blood. Jimmy says that's just the female thing, but I don't know, man.

Mom takes the phone and chatters with Grandma in Spanish.

"Don't worry about it, Mom, they won't deport you," she says in English, sitting down in front of the television. I look up from punching a baseball in my glove. *Deport*. That is a word a lot of people have been tossing around lately. "You have been in the country for over thirty years. They won't just deport you now," she says again, rolling her eyes.

I can hear Grandma going on in Spanish, superfast. Mom listens while watching the demonstrations in Arizona. Sometimes she watches Fox News with the blond-haired dude who says we have to deport all the illegals. It makes you get kind of scared because you wonder if they'll be able to tell who is who. Mom leans forward with the phone.

"Nothing is going to happen," she says again in a low voice.

"It will get struck down in the courts."

But I don't think Grandma is buying it. I can hear her voice and Mom is rolling through the channels again. "Just go to the grocery store like you always have," she tells her, moving an ashtray across the table. "No one will bother you."

Grandma chatters so much, Mom shoots through three different channels. A man who looks like George Lopez stands in front of a microphone. "Are we going to allow our civil liberties to be stripped away? Are we going to allow police to use Gestapo tactics against us because of the color of our skin?" Grandma talks loud enough where I can hear the whole conversation.

"How's Ricky?"

"He's playing baseball," Mom answers, looking at me.

"And he is pitching the ball?"

"Yeah, but I need to get him some coaching for the high school tryouts," Mom says, leaning close to the television.

"And how will you do that?"

"There is a man across the street who might help us."

"He is a coach?"

"A pitcher."

Grandma switches to Spanish and I go to get a glass of milk. On the refrigerator Mom has this quote she cut out and taped up: *A coach not only has to teach the fundamentals, but he must also instruct the young player on the philosophy of the pitcher. In this way he teaches the pitcher a way to be.* I turn with my milk and polish off some chocolate cake on the kitchen table. I stare at the light beneath the Pitcher's garage and think about *"a way to be."* I always liked the last part of that quote.

I finish my milk and go back where Mom still has the phone to her ear. I sit down on our couch that is real saggy and great for sacking out on after hours of ESPN. I love the way those dudes yell at each other over who's the MVP for a game or whether a guy may be suspended because he blew off practice. Their shouting drives Mom crazy and she's always telling me to turn it down. But to me, man, it's like music.

"How is your health, Maria?"

"Fine, Mom. I'm fine."

"Are you still smoking?'

"I quit, Mom," she says, picking up her Marlboros.

They switch back to Spanish and then she hangs up and lights her cigarette. It's funny. I lie to Mom about my homework and she lies to her Mom about smoking. I guess when you get down to it, *everyone* lies to their parents. She clicks away the television and tells me to go to bed. I brush my teeth and throw on my Zambrano jersey. Then I go out to the living room and Mom's out on the porch having her before-bed smoke. I walk up and stand behind the screen.

I can hear the crickets and the airy sound of the Pitcher's ballgame. Mom is staring across the street. She slowly puts the cigarette to her lips, keeping her eyes on his garage.

7

MOM CHECKS OUT A BUNCH of books from the library and sits at our kitchen table making notes. *Nolan Ryan's Pitcher's Bible, The Picture Perfect Pitcher, The Art of Pitching.* We go out to the field behind Roland School. Mom tells me how to hold the ball and set myself while she catches with all the gear. I ring the backstop, firing the ball right over her head. I just don't have control and most times we go home more discouraged than when we began. The tryouts are getting closer and I think Mom really knows pitching can't be taught from a book. I think that's why she signed me up for the camp.

It's this one-day camp at the high school run by the coaches and the word is they are using it to weed kids out. It cost two hundred bucks for one day. We never did the camps because we just couldn't afford them. But everybody who's trying out for the high school team has signed up.

Mom drives me over in the morning and in the parking lot are all these Escalades and Land Rovers and a few Hummers. A lot of people in Jacksonville are loaded. Mom stubs her cigarette, staring toward the field.

"Ready?"

I stare at the blond-haired boys milling around with new bats, gloves, and bright new bat bags. It looks like a convention of rich white boys to me. I'm thinking about our rusted-out minivan with the hubcaps missing. I breathe heavily, fingering my bat bag with the broken zipper. I look up and see Eric and his dad talking to two men with SOUTH HIGH SCHOOL on their red shirts.

"It's only camp. It's not the tryouts," Mom says, staring at the coaches.

"They'll remember who's good," I murmur.

"That's why you are going to show them what Ricky Hernandez can do!"

I turn to Mom, who looks really Mexican with her curly black hair pulled back in her cap. She's wearing her Marauders jersey and I wish she hadn't. I wish she was wearing the shorts or the cool sunglasses like other moms wear. Instead she has on her Oakleys that make her look kind of weird.

"Other boys throw fast too."

Mom pulls down her sunglasses and leans in.

"That's why you are here—to learn, right?"

"I'm here to get my butt kicked," I mutter, opening the door.

We get out and I have my uniform on. Word is you should wear your uniform to show you are on a team, but *nobody* has a uniform on. Mom goes over to find out if we need to check in. Then I see Eric walking toward me with a bat over his shoulder, looking like an MLB pitcher.

"Hey, *beano,* you don't usually come to these camps," he says like we are best friends.

I hate that word. *Beano.*

"Yeah ... s*o!*"

Eric lowers his bat and gnashes on his gum, then takes off his hat and smooths back his blond crew. He puts his hand on my shoulder. "Look dude, if I were you, I would stress your catching abilities," he says like he's doing me this big favor. "Then you might at least have a chance. I mean you are a little *screwy* in the head to pitch, right?"

I think he's talking about when I pulled the knife on him. The word was that I was like a psycho dude, which I'm not. But that's the press release Eric put out there and it was all just to make sure *he's* the pitcher.

I open my bat bag and pull out my mitt.

"I'm a pitcher," I tell him.

Eric snorts and laughs and makes all these weird faces. He claps me on the shoulder again like we are best friends. "Dude, you may have an arm, but the competition is really stiff. I mean you can't even get it over the *plate* half the time! You don't have a curve or a sinker and you don't have a change-up."

"And you can't throw a fastball over fifty," I reply, shrugging.

Then I see Mrs. Payne marching toward us like a general. She glares at me like I'm infecting her son or something.

"Eric! Get over here!"

He rolls the gum between his teeth and spits in the grass.

"Well, gotta go meet my future coach, dude," he says, putting his bat on his shoulder. "But look, just try and do well in the batting practice. I mean you have all that experience, man, swatting piñatas ... right?"

Now we're under the hot sun where two coaches in red Polo shirts stand outside the dugout. Coach Hoskins is big and bald and announces, "This is high school baseball, boys, and nothing you will do will ever be more important than right now. This is the first opportunity to get noticed." I like Coach Hoskins. He seems like an old-time coach with a big gut and a smile. I'm hoping he's going to be the freshman coach.

"Alright. I want to introduce you to our new freshman coach, Coach Poppers." He steps back and this younger guy with a Marine haircut steps up. He's got this flattop buzz like something you see in the movies. We all listen because he is *the dude*, the freshman coach. He starts talking about how making the freshman team will set you up for playing on the varsity and all, and then he starts talking about pitching.

"Baseball has changed. It is about performance and that requires a rigorous attention to mechanics. This is for you pitchers. I can slow down someone's motion in my laptop and tell them exactly what they are doing wrong. If they follow my instructions, then they will improve, but if you want to be a rebel or be some old-time wildman ..." he pauses, his blue eyes landing on each of us, "I have no use for you. Pitching is not an art, it is a science."

I groan inwardly, because science is my worst subject. And I can tell this dude is not going to be down with a Mexican pitcher. He is like "all Eric." I mean they even look alike! Mom says the color of your skin doesn't matter. She says you just hold your head up and look everyone in the eye. I don't know about that with Coach Poppers.

"Now, I want you all to line up for cup inspection," he announces. We form a line while Coach Poppers walks with a bat. He stops and squints down the line like a cop. "Everyone is wearing a cup, right?"

And then he swings his bat into Lance's crotch and you hear the *tink* of his cup. I'm sweating because I forgot my cup. Alright, I didn't forget it, I lost it. It was always popping up in the laundry or under my bed. One time it ended up in the front yard. Don't ask me how. Coach Poppers is walking down the line and tapping every kid in the crotch. Sometimes the bat goes *tink* and sometimes the kid just bends over and turns white.

"Let this be a lesson to you boys who forgot your cup. You never know when I'm going to have cup inspection," he shouts after knocking half of the kids in the nuts. "Alright, let's break up into pitchers and fielders."

I breathe in relief. Eric looks at me and frowns.

"What, you forget your cup?"

I shrug and he scoffs.

"Cups are for fags, beano," he says. "So you better get yours."

I stare at him. I mean, what can you say to a dude like that?

They divide us between pitchers and outfielders and the two coaches go off to the dugout. I don't have a good feeling about this Don Poppers dude with his iPhone and super-white socks. He doesn't look like he digs kids with bat bags that don't zip who drive up in rusted-out minivans.

These college guys called counselors all wear wraparound Oakleys, sport small goatees, and chew gum. Some have tobacco in their lips and spit all over the place. They wear shiny red-and-white jerseys with their old numbers. Already whispers of *That's Connor Albright man; he pitches for Duke* have started. I line up with the pitchers as Connor flips over a bucket and sits down behind home plate. No gear, nothing. He pounds his worn glove, making dust clouds.

"Bring it to me. Give me your best!"

The word is the counselors tell the coaches who the standouts are. Eric is already talking to Connor, who is a blond-haired dude too. I'm the only Mexican I can see so far.

"Just give me three of your best," Connor yells again from his white bucket.

My heart is banging away in my chest. The first three pitchers throw wild, sending balls high and into the dirt. This makes me feel better. If I screw up I will at least have some company. Connor gets off his bucket and pulls us into a huddle. He spits into the dust, then speaks in a low baseball voice.

"Alright, listen," he begins, going down to one knee. "I don't want you guys to be all freaked out. This is a camp and yes there is some evaluating going on, but this is just a camp. So calm down and just bring it to me. OK?" Connor goes back to his bucket and adjusts his Oakleys, smacking his glove again.

"Alright, let's go!"

The next pitcher throws in three fastballs. The following pitchers bring in decent curves, fastballs, and sinkers. Connor nods for some boys while others he just calls out, "*Next!*" I close my eyes and say a prayer, but I can't really stay focused. When I get stressed my mind goes off like a rocket. Like right now I'm thinking about Pete Rose and wondering if he will ever get in the Hall of Fame. I mean, who would think about that right before they pitch?

Eric throws a fastball, a curve, and a beautiful cutter. Connor nods to him and yells, "Nice pitching, Eric!" I shut my eyes. The dude *knows his name* already! It's my turn and Eric flips the ball to me with this little grin.

"It's not too late to go try out with the catchers," he snickers.

I take the ball that feels heavy in my hand. Connor pounds out dust from his mitt.

"C'mon ... bring it here!"

My hands are sweaty and I can't keep them dry enough to grip the ball. I look down from the pitcher's mound with my heart pounding this rhythm of, *Right now, right now, right now.* I close my eyes and feel Mom watching from the stands. I'm so nervous, I'm not even breathing right. Connor hits his glove again.

"Bring it on. C'mon, bring it to me here!"

I shut my eyes and figure I have one chance to bring the heat. I open my eyes and position a three-finger grip, set myself, take my breath, then kick into my windup. I put everything I have into that pitch, but I know right away my release is wrong. Connor sees the wild pitch and scoops low as the ball hammers his ankle. I've never seen someone jump straight off a bucket and scream like that. He curses, hobbling around like a man in a one-legged race. My face is burning as the other pitchers stare at me. I had just nailed the counselor in the ankle with a fastball.

Connor limps back and sets his bucket back up. I have two more pitches, but he picks up his mitt and glares at me. He shakes his head and shouts, *"NEXT!"*

MOM NEVER GIVES UP. SHE never gave up when my third grade teacher said I was behind in reading. She bought *Hooked on Phonics* and we listened to it every night. Or when it came to math ... she made up flash cards and taught me multiplication on the stairs of our porch. Same with pitching. Mom read every book in the world on pitching. I saw her trying to master the three-finger and two-finger grip in her bedroom. Sometimes she would burst into tears because she just couldn't get it. So it doesn't surprise me when she walks out with the plate of fajitas.

"Come on," she says, walking down the porch steps.

I follow her as she holds the fajitas like a waiter.

"Where are we going?"

"The way to a man's heart is through his stomach," she explains as we walk up his drive.

Mom has put on lipstick, heels, and a tight blue dress. She walks with that purpose that makes her jiggle all over, her hoop earrings swinging. I can smell perfume mixing with the sautéed onions and green peppers. She stops outside the garage and breathes deeply, then raps on the door with her knuckles.

"Mr. Langford!"

I hear the ballgame. Someone gets a hit and the crowd roars. Mom stands there with the napkin-covered plate. The onions smell great. She wipes the corner of her mouth, dabbing the lipstick on the back of her dress. Shortstop looks out from under the garage, sniffing the air.

"Maybe he already ate, Mom," I mutter.

"Then he can eat again. Mr. Langford! I brought you some dinner!"

The ballgame turns down like someone had thrown a blanket over it. I hear those halting steps again, then I smell his cigarette. Mom shifts her weight and tosses back her curly hair. She looks at me with the blue dress making her eyes sparkle. Then there is no sound at all and I don't hear his shoes anymore.

"I don't think he's coming, Mom," I whisper.

"Mr. Langford. I am going to put these fajitas under the door," Mom calls loudly. "I hope your dog doesn't get them!"

She pauses and I hope he will at least say *something*. Mom went to a lot of trouble to get dressed up and bring him food. She looks at me as if to say, *well what else can I do?* She rolls her shoulders, then puts the plate down and slides it inside. Shortstop follows the fajitas closely. I know they're going to end up in his stomach. We start down the drive and that's when the garage starts clanking.

From his pictures I'm thinking a Roger Clemens dude. On YouTube he looks really tall. In real life, I stare at this meaty guy with a barrel chest, large nose, and lined grey eyes. His grey hair is greased straight back. The Pitcher's eyes remind me of a hawk, the way he watches us. He continues smoking with the cigarette behind his hand.

Mom picks up the plate that Shortstop is sniffing.

"Do you like fajitas, Mr. Langford?"

The Pitcher pauses, then drops his cigarette and stubs it with his old loafer. He has on baggy shorts and a golf shirt with a pack of Pall Malls in his top pocket. Mom pulls back the napkin and he picks up one of the fajitas.

"Mr. Langford," she says, handing him a napkin, "my son needs a pitching coach. He has the arm, but he needs someone who can take him to the next level." Mom pauses, pulling back her hair. "I will pay you to coach my son and get him ready for the high school tryouts."

He takes another bite of the fajita, his bloodshot eyes on Mom.

"I told you," he mutters, swallowing, "I ain't no coach, lady."

Mom whips up a roll of twenties from her dress like a dealer.

"I have a hundred dollars here for his first lesson," she says, holding out the slim tube. I know how hard it was for Mom to scrape that up. It may only be a hundred bucks to him, but to us it is like *a thousand*. The Pitcher doesn't say anything and Mom just stands there with the money, wind blowing her hair over one eye, her lip still swollen from Fernando.

"Thanks for the food," he says, putting back the fajita. "But I ain't coaching your kid. I don't coach nobody."

Then he steps back and pulls out his garage remote. The garage starts clanking down and that's when Mom *stuffs* the hundred dollars in his shirt pocket.

"That's for his first lesson!" she shouts as the door swallows him up.

Then Mom turns and clacks down the drive in her heels. She's almost running as we beat it back to our house. We go inside and she turns around and looks through the window. Mom lights a cigarette and lifts the curtain again, staring at the garage. She breathes heavily and looks at me with her spiked heels up on the couch.

"Do you think I freaked him out?"

"Oh yeah," I reply. But really, Mom freaks out just about everybody.

9

I HEAR MOM ON THE phone with some lady from the bank. I don't eat another bite of my mac and cheese. It's some sort of program from President Obama. The president's plan doesn't look like it's going to help us now, because Mom presses her head against the fridge. A lot of people in our neighborhood have lost their homes. You can tell because their grass gets real long and trash ends up in the front yard. Usually the For Sale sign is stolen and a couple windows are broken. So I know Mom is thinking we're going to end up with trash in our yard and our windows cracked.

We get these calls for Mom's medical bills. They flash up on our television and we just sit there and wait for the calls to stop. Then we keep watching like it never happened. But she always has the bills out on the kitchen table. I know since she lost her health insurance, she quit going to the doctors. I mean it's like thousands and I don't know how she's ever going to pay that. But she always says where there is a will there is a way.

I don't move while her head presses against the refrigerator. She stays that way for a long minute, then lifts her head and looks at me. She smiles and tries to put the mom-spin on it. "We'll figure out something," she says brightly, like we had been having this conversation. Mom just doesn't like to show she's worried. "C'mon, let's go practice your pitching."

And then she wipes her eyes and walks onto the porch.

So now Mom is crouched down in the street. Everything smells like oil because the street gets so hot during the day and the tar melts. Our neighbors, the Newtons, have this pit bull they keep tied up to their porch and he's barking like he wants to kill somebody. It's been like a week since Mom gave the Pitcher the hundred bucks. I figured he blew it on Good Times beer by now. I wait while Mom sets herself and brings her mitt up. She looks smaller in the chest protector and face mask with her hat on backward. It's still hot at seven o'clock and I know she's sweating in the shin guards and the black foam chest shield.

"Alright. I want to see this one from the windup!"

I hold the ball down and feel like I'm being watched.

"Mom ... can't we go to a field?"

"No. Pitch it here," she calls, beating her mitt.

I pull in and go into my set.

"Don't forget to breathe!"

"*Mom!*" I shout, breaking my hands. "Don't say anything when I'm pitching, alright?"

She holds up the catcher's glove.

"C'mon ... enough talk ... pitch it here, Zambrano!"

The Newton dog is going crazy. The dog's bark is going right through my skull. Some guys can pitch through anything, but I got to find the quiet place. And there ain't nothing quiet about the Newton's pit bull. I set myself again, then kick back into my windup, coming over with a fastball. The ball soars over Mom's head, skipping down the street. She goes clanking after it, running halfway back, then pulls off the mask.

"Now what did you do wrong there?" she asks, breathing hard.

"You're the coach, you tell me," I mutter.

Mom's eyes narrow and spark.

"Hey! What's with the attitude?"

I hold out my hands because I know why we're in the street. I know she's trying to get the Pitcher to come out of his garage. But that dude is not coming out. No way. He got a hundred bucks for nothing.

"This is *stupid!* You don't know what you're doing!"

Mom snaps her finger at me.

"Enough of that! We can figure this out together!" She holds the catcher's mask beneath her arm. "I think you're breathing wrong. What do you think?"

"Oh really? What Internet site did you read that off of?"

She jabs her finger at me.

"Look, *jerko*, I'm doing this for you!"

"Maybe I don't want you to do it for me!"

I don't know why I say half the stuff I do, but sometimes I just get mad for no reason. I know the Pitcher will never coach me. I get that. So let's just go to Roland Field where at least I won't hit a car or something. But Mom can't take *no* from anybody. So I walk up to her and lean forward, speaking low.

"He's not coming back out ... this is *stupid.*"

"Don't be an ass, Ricky." She pulls down her mask. "Now shut up and pitch!"

"Shut up and pitch, shut up and pitch," I mimic.

"Keep it up and you'll find yourself with no ESPN for a week."

"Big deal," I grumble, walking back down the street.

Mom hits her catcher's mitt again. It's then I feel this rage. It's the same rage I felt when they put me with the fielders at the camp. I let fly an inside fastball that bounces up into Mom's chest protector. She falls back like she's dead.

"Mom, Mom ... are you alright?"

She nods and pushes herself up slowly.

"I like the speed. Let's just put in my mitt next time."

I feel a great relief. "Let's not do this, Mom. I don't want to bean you again."

She frowns.

"That's why I have the gear. Now get back down the street!"

But that's when I see her wince. She's been doing that a lot lately. Mom turns real white and I ask her if something's wrong. I've noticed she's tired, sleeping a lot on the couch and picking at her food. When I ask her about the calls from the doctor, she always says it's nothing.

"Mom, listen, maybe we should take a break."

Her eyes start doing this trapped butterfly thing, moving side-to-side. Then her chin starts bobbing. She can go real ethnic when she wants to.

"Bullshit, *cabrón.*" She throws me the ball. "Get your butt down there and throw me a fastball."

So I walk back down the street, pacing off the feet. I turn and Mom is squatting again, pounding her mitt.

"Bring it, Carlos."

10

WE PLAY IN THE STREET all week. Mom brings out another diagram on how to throw a curve, a sinker, a change-up. Sometimes, the wind blows the paper while she tries to figure out the grip. Sometimes she gets it. Sometimes she screams and cusses.

On the last night, it is getting dark with the bungalows shadowing the street. I throw some pitches that zing like guided missiles. I have just caught the ball from Mom when I hear the clanking of his garage door.

The garage goes up slowly and the Pitcher appears in a lawn chair with a six-pack of Good Times beer. Shortstop is slumped next to him. It's like a game show the way he is sitting there and smoking a cigarette. He pops a beer without saying a word. Mom looks at me and shrugs, then hunches down. I'm really nervous. I go into my windup and nothing feels right. I come over the top and release high and the ball soars over her head. Mom clanks down the street in her catcher gear like the Tin Man. The Pitcher just smokes and looks really bored.

That's the way it goes. I keep throwing wild and Mom keeps chasing the balls down the street. The Pitcher sits there with his dog and watches me pitch. When it is almost dark, the garage goes back down.

***

Mom got some books from the library and lays them open on her bed. I watch while the ball falls from her hand as she tries to get the grip. I'm not sure pitching can be taught from a book. To me pitching is like something that comes out after dark, you know. Like when the land turns that funny grey color and everything is quiet and a few black birds dart across the horizon. That's what pitching feels like when it's right—a moment before all that darkness.

Mom is trying to learn it from the outside, which is what you do if you've never pitched. You think it can just be taught from a book like math or science or history. But I think it's more like English where Mrs. Gibbons says words stand for other things. Like a sunset is not just a sunset, but something about death. Or a sunrise is about birth. Same thing with pitching; a fastball isn't just a fastball—it's who you are. Some people get it, most don't.

But this change-up, I don't know, man. Mom has left her bedroom, and we are back in the street. Mom is shouting all these instructions.

"Just throw it slower," she says, hunching down.

"I think it's more complicated than that," I shout back.

"Just do it and throw me a change-up!"

I see her glance toward the Pitcher in his lawn chair a couple times. The dude watches us about every night and hasn't tried to give Mom back her hundred bucks. That's pretty crappy of him. I mean, now we are entertaining him and he still has our money! All he does is sit there and drink beers.

Mom gets back into position and beats her mitt.

"C'mon, bring it to me, Ricky!"

I pitch what I think might be a change-up. Mom manages to snag the wild pitch before it disappears down the street and I feel my face getting hot. Here is this major league pitcher watching and I can't get *any* control. Mom stands there and I can tell she doesn't know what to say either.

"So what did you do wrong?" she asks, walking up out of breath.

"I told you I don't know what I'm doing," I say in a low voice. "This is stupid! You don't know how to pitch and I don't—"

Mom whips out the printout from her pocket. "I don't think you are taking your breath properly. You have to take a deep breath before you pitch."

"I'm taking my fricking breath, Mom."

"Come here and let me see you do it," she commands. "I want to see a really big breath. C'mon, right now."

I feel my face burning up.

"This is stupid."

"Shut up and breathe in. This is probably why you can't throw a change-up."

"Breathing has nothing to do with it, Mom!"

"Shut up and breathe! We'll do it together. Ready? One, two, three!"

So I do. I mean once Mom sets her eye on something there is no getting away. And I see us. These two Mexicans in the street breathing like they are on oxygen or something. I just want to hide, man. My face is burning hot. I take a deep breath with Mom facing me. We are now right in front of the Pitcher.

"Again!"

We breathe in the street like two fish. Mom's cheeks are full and her mouth forms an "o". I see the Pitcher shaking his head slowly. He uncrosses his leg and stares at us like we have just crapped in the street.

"OK," Mom says loudly. "Now let it out and in again and let it out and in again."

"Mom, I'm not breathing anymore!" I shout.

She whips out the printout and I hear the Pitcher's chair scrape the pavement.

"Jesus Christ," he mutters, standing up and I figure he's going to leave the two Mexican nuts in the street. Mom glances at him and says real loud, "It says here, Ricky, before every pitch you have to breathe!"

"I'm not breathing anymore."

"You will breathe!" Mom shouts.

I hear the Pitcher walking then, his hard shoes on the street. He is striding toward Mom and she turns as he pulls the printout from her hand. She faces him with her mouth open, her cheeks red. The Pitcher tears the printout in two.

"You expect me to listen to this shit for a hundred lousy bucks?"

Mom looks at him.

"No. I expect you to coach my son."

"Jesus Christ," he mutters, throwing his cigarette in the street. The Pitcher looks at Mom and shakes his head. "Lady, you got a lot of brass."

Mom stares back with the catcher's mask under her arm.

"I don't have a choice."

The Pitcher breathes heavily.

"Alright ..." he says wearily, gesturing down the street. "Go down and catch so I can watch your son pitch!"

"What about breathing?"

"Breathing don't have a goddamn thing to do with pitching!"

"That's not what the printout says," she murmurs.

"Lady, I don't give a good damn what the printout says," he declares. "Now get on down there so your son can pitch to you!"

Mom hesitates, then winks at me and walks down the street. She turns around under the low moon. The Pitcher stands in the half-light, his eyes picking me out of the dusk.

"Now forget about the goddamn breathing and pick a spot," he orders.

I stare at him with the ripped printout blowing down the street.

"*Well* ...What the hell are you doing?"

I shrug. "Pitching?"

"Then pitch the goddamn ball!"

I bring my arms in but my hands are shaking. My entire body is shaking or something, because here is the thing: I have never really had a pitching lesson. Everything I know about pitching I've seen on television. The rest is God-given, as Mom always says. So I just stand there, trembling in the warm Florida night, trying to get my grip straight.

"Hold it ..." the Pitcher raises his hand. "Do you have a spot?"

"What?"

He puts a cigarette in his mouth and cracks open a silver lighter.

"*A spot* ... you need a spot if you are going to pitch, rockhead." He puts the lighter back in his pocket, pointing his cigarette toward Mom. "You have to find a spot to aim for or you're going to throw it all over hell the way you been doing. I used to pick the batter's wrist. Why don't you concentrate on your Mom's glove."

I set myself again. The trembling is still there, but my legs don't feel like jelly anymore. The Pitcher stands to the side, smoking. He leans forward.

"What the hell are you waiting for ... the second coming? *Pitch!*"

I take my breath and kick back, launching the ball clear over Mom's head. I had released too high, but I was so jacked up. I wait while Mom turns to get the ball. The Pitcher pulls the cigarette from his mouth.

"Hey ... *whaddaya doing?*"

"What?"

He points down the street with his cigarette.

"Don't make your Mom get it ... *go get the goddamn ball!*"

I take off and sprint by Mom. I run back out of breath and turn around. The Pitcher sparks his cigarette again.

"Alright, let's see it from the stretch. Only this time aim for your mother's mitt instead of the goddamn moon."

I tug on my hat and look down. I try to concentrate on Mom's mitt, but the ball flies out of my hand all wrong. It flares under the streetlight and sails over her head. The Pitcher pulls out a can of Skoal.

"Hurry up. I ain't got all night while you pitch for the rooftops."

I grab the ball again and come huffing back. Every time I reach him I am relieved he is still there. The Pitcher purses his lips and nods to me. "Alright ... that one just hit the trees. Let's try it again. Bring it *down* this time," he orders, pointing the star of his cigarette. "You're releasing too goddamn early. You gotta follow through." He spits tobacco juice into the street and looks at me. "Look, rockhead, you ever hit somebody?"

"Well ... yeah."

The Pitcher cocks back his arm and then comes forward. "Well think of hitting a man," he explains, making a fist. "You gotta follow through like you're punching somebody. You understand that? You gotta follow through with your pitch like you just slugged the hell out of somebody. You think you can do that?"

"I think so."

"Alright. Try it from the windup and don't aim for the moon ... aim for her *glove.*"

I set myself and keep my eye on Mom's glove. I take a breath, kick back, and whip the ball over the top. I release too high again, but Mom manages to grab it. The Pitcher rifles the warm tar again with tobacco juice and waves his hand.

"Alright, now let's see your fastball."

I pull in to my set, but throw high again. When I come back he begins adjusting me: I wasn't stepping off right. I didn't have my shoulder square. I wasn't pushing off my right foot. I throw three more really bad pitches. Nothing is working the way it should. So that's why I ask him this: "Can I try one pitch my way now?"

The Pitcher stares at me and frowns.

"Your way ain't working, rockhead."

"You haven't let me do it my way."

"Yeah. Sure. Then do it your way."

I take a deep breath and close my eyes. I hear the wind and keep my eyes closed until everything is still. I set myself, then open my eyes on Mom's mitt. I draw back with my arm and snap down like a mousetrap. The ball cracks into Mom's mitt. It was still high, but it was my fastball.

I turn and the Pitcher is staring at me.

"Can you do that again?"

"Yeah, maybe."

Of course the next one flies over Mom's head, but he sees it. Kind of like the way you see lightning sometimes and even though there is no rain, you know a storm is coming.

Mom pulls off her mask and we meet under the streetlight. The Pitcher breathes out smoke and looks at me. I can hear the crickets and a distant train. He holds up a big finger.

"Alright," he begins slowly. "The first thing you gotta know is the whole world is a full count against you. You understand what I'm saying?"

"Yes, sir," I reply. "I think so."

"Call me Jack. What I'm saying is no one will bail you out. You are all alone on the mound and it's all stacked against you. You gotta prove yourself with every pitch."

"Yes, sir."

He taps his cigarette toward me like a baton.

"After that, you gotta pick a spot. If you don't pick a spot, then you can't pitch. Like I said, I used to aim for the batter's wrist. I figured if I broke their wrist, so much the better. Sometimes I'd see a hole or something in the back wall and I'd pick that. It don't matter." He pistols his finger. " But you gotta have a spot."

"Yes, sir."

"Call me Jack."

"Yes, sir, sir ... I mean yes, sir ... I mean, Jack."

The Pitcher looks at Mom.

"Does he always talk like this?"

"Just when one of his dreams comes true," Mom answers, her eyes getting wet.

He drops his cigarette in the street.

"You on a team now?"

"Yeah, the Marauders."

"They have a game tomorrow on Pearson Field, six o'clock," Mom says quickly.

The Pitcher nods, then pulls the rolled twenties from his pocket.

"That's for his first lesson," Mom says, backing away.

The Pitcher looks at her in the darkness.

"Lady, if I charged you for lessons, it'd be a hell of a lot more than a hundred bucks," he says, putting the money in her hand.

Then he picks up his can of beer and walks back to his lawn chair. We stand there as the garage clanks back down. Mom turns to me, her eyes glistening.

"You might have a coach, Ricky," she whispers.

"Yeah," I say, picking up the pieces of the printout from the street. I squint at the torn paper and read. "Hey, Mom, this is on that law in Arizona." I frown, looking at her. "There's nothing here about baseball, or breathing."

Mom blinks twice, her eyebrows going up.

"Really?"

11

THERE ARE THESE GUYS WHO come to every game. Mom and I call them the gang of three. They are guys who figure going to baseball games is better than doing anything else. They sit in their folding chairs and holler and drink from a thermos with plastic cups. SIT DOWN! HE CAN'T PITCH! HE SUCKS! They eat peanuts from a clear plastic bag and have big guts and goatees. Everyone tries to ignore them, but they can really mess up your game.

I am on the mound, using what the Pitcher told me about picking a spot and following through. I look for him every time I take the ball from the catch. Mom says to forget about the Pitcher and just concentrate on the game, but I can't help looking toward the outfield fence. Maybe worrying about the Pitcher is the reason things are starting to go bad—that and the gang of three.

To pitch well you have to concentrate. It's like the whole

world has to go away and it's just you and the batter. That's what the Pitcher told me out in the street. I turn on the mound and wipe my brow and size up the batter. "HE CAN'T PITCH! HE AIN'T GOT NO ARM!" I stare at the three guys in their lawn chairs. The funny sounds that reach you on the mound always amaze me. *Stop it, Johnny! Get him, Ricky! No more pizza, I told you! They can't hit!* It's like a radio with all these different stations on at once. But the gang of three drowns out everybody else. I remember them from the last time we played the Yankees. They shouted every time one of our players came up to bat.

"HE SUCKS. HE'S TAKING A DIVE. GO HOME!"

We are tied with the Yankees in the sixth after Eric shut them down. I think Devin figured I could take some heat off their order with my speed. The Yankees' batters just stand there because their coaches just give them the take sign. They must figure I'm wild so they'll wait me out and get a walk. Not tonight. I mowed down the first batter with three fastballs. The second batter is when the gang of three started in on me. I could never quite get the balk thing straight in my head. Was it breaking your hands from the set position? Moving your foot off the rubber? Every umpire seemed to have a different interpretation.

"BALK!"

The gang of three yell it every time I start to move. Or they yell, "HE CAN'T PITCH!" or "HE'S GOT NO ARM!" It's like the second I break my hands they start yelling. Even the umpire turns around and stares at them. Then I start throwing highfliers and some into the dirt. The gang of three goes crazy and start yelling, "HE SUCKS! HE SUCKS!" Then Blue calls me on a balk.

"Balk! Advance a base."

I have runners on first and second and the gang of three is laying it on. In baseball games it's all about momentum and the crowd sniffs who has it. They figure they have me on the ropes now. A kid with an arm can destroy a team, but if they make that kid lose his mind, then he's nothing.

"HE CAN'T PITCH!"

"HE DOESN'T KNOW HOW TO PITCH!"

"GO SIT DOWN!"

"THE PITCHER SUCKS!"

I see Mom pacing back and forth and yelling something at these guys. They just smile and raise their cups. Once these guys get a coach to start arguing, they've succeeded. I can see Mom is really pissed. I take a deep breath and try to push it all away. I see the third base coach give a run of signals and feel a steal coming. But the gang of three isn't going to let me off that easy.

"C'MON, PITCH THE BALL ... QUIT SLOWING THE GAME."

I set myself, turning my head slightly, and see the runner off second. Artie, the second baseman, starts to drift over. That's when I move my foot off the rubber and break my hands and pivot.

"YOU SUCK!" the gang of three scream as the runner bolts for third. I turn and overthrow Ronnie at third and the runner sprints for home. I run to the plate to back up the throw, but it's too late. The Yankee scores and the three guys stand up and yell together, "SIT DOWN!"

And that's when I hear it, man. Like something rotten in a cooler that nearly knocks you over. Right after *SIT DOWN!* the fat guy in the middle in the T-shirt with cutoff sleeves stands up and yells, "GO BACK TO MEXICO, YOU WETBACK!"

The words are like someone just punched the air out of me. My face starts burning. Now I'm the Mexican on the mound because everyone heard him. Then my eyes tear up. I see Mom running toward these dudes. She is on fire. She runs with her hair flying back and the fat guy with the goatee stands up and lifts his arms. He yells out like a Viking, holding up his cup. Mom grabs a bat from the ground and the guy spreads his arms out.

"Oh the *beano mom* is going to hit with me with a bat?" He laughs and looks at the other guys. "Why don't you put that bat down, lady, before you hurt somebody."

Mom stares at him, then puts the Louisville Slugger down.

"That's right lady, you ain't going to do anything," he says, grinning, looking at the other guys.

Mom walks up to the dude. The guy is in flip flops and I hear his voice the way you can hear someone talking at night.

"What ... you going to take a punch now?"

"No," Mom says.

She then lifts her cleat and stomps down hard on his bare foot. The dude screams in this high-pitched voice and falls to the ground. I know it hurt, man. I've been spiked before and I wasn't barefoot. He's crying, holding his foot like a giant baby. Mom swings up the bat and the other two guys stand up out of their chairs.

"Who else called my son a wetback?!" she shouts at them.

Those guys stand there like statues, man, while the guy cries on the ground. Mom tells them to get the hell out of there and they do. And everybody is watching, man. That's when I turn and see this big dude leaning on the outfield fence in sunglasses. He's standing by himself with his long arms resting on the steel grey piping. He puts a cigarette to his mouth like he's seen it all before.

12

I STRUGGLE TO GET THE batting equipment into our minivan. The sun has gone down behind the trees and the infields glow against the grass. We are the last to leave because Mom always makes sure the dugout is cleaned up and we throw away Gatorade bottles and empty packages of seeds and gum and baggies of peanut shells. We have to take the big black dusty equipment bag, which is really heavy. I have just gotten the bag of batting helmets and catcher gear in the back of our van when I feel someone behind me.

I turn to the Pitcher standing in the parking lot with his glasses on. He smokes the way someone might waiting for a train.

"You know where Roland Field is?"

"Yeah."

"See you there at eight. "

And then he just walks off across the lot like a ghost. I feel like I have just made the Chicago Cubs. I run up to the front of the van.

"He was here, Mom! He's going to coach me!"

She stares at me then tears out of the van. Mom looks around the empty parking lot, but there are just some kids playing catch by their car. Mom turns and stares at me.

"I'm so happy for you, Ricky."

She starts to cry. Nothing new there. Mom cries over movies, television shows, even commercials. Mom says her nickname was "bawler" when she was a kid. Go figure.

***

So now I'm walking through the dewy grass across the field by the Roland School. Mom is watching me like I'm a five-year-old going to kindergarten for the first time. I keep walking with my bat bag on my shoulder. The grass is sparkling wet and my cleats are swishing like skis. It's my first lesson with the Pitcher and I'm jacked. I walk up to the baseball diamond Mom and I practiced on and hear this low rumbling. I see a cleat in the dugout and then a leg next to three cans of Good Times. The Pitcher snores on the bench like he's going to throw up.

Yeah, man, my coach. I stare at him with my bag on my shoulder. I mean, do you just wake a World Series pitcher up or do you let him sleep? He keeps snoring and rumbling like some kind of volcano. I barely slept all night and got up around five and sat in the kitchen with my bat bag. But now I feel like one of those balloons that whip all over the room when the air runs out. I sit down on the bench and watch him for a while, his lips creating weird noises like some kind of sea creature.

Finally, I lean over.

"Mr. Langford?"

He pauses, then keeps snoring, his lips smacking together. I watch his stomach and try to calculate how many Good Times beers have gone into that mountain. I sit for a few minutes. I either go home or wake him up and I don't want to go back home. So I lean over and got pretty close to his ear.

"MR. LANGFORD!"

His eyes blink open like a dead guy. The Pitcher wipes the drool off his mouth and squints at me. He hacks into the dust, going, "ahhhhh," like he just had a great nap.

"You don't gotta yell," he grumbles, sitting up.

"I didn't think you'd wake up."

He kicks away his beer cans and spits globs in the dirt. The Pitcher fishes his cigarettes out and squints out to the infield.

"Must have fallen asleep," he mutters, pulling on his cigarette.

I stare at my hands with my bat bag on my shoulder. The Pitcher stands up, then looks at me like he's surprised I'm still here.

"Why don't you jog around the field a few times," he says, motioning with his cigarette.

"How many times?"

"Four should be good."

I stare at the big field and frown.

"You got a problem with that, rockhead?"

I mumble, "No," and then start off in a light jog.

I have always hated running. I have long legs and arms and nothing seems to move the way it is supposed to. And it's just stupid because there are lots of fat pitchers who can't run. The grass is wet and my shoes are soaked after one lap. I finish and walk back across the infield and into the dugout. The Pitcher is lying down, snoring like he never stopped.

***

"You got a baseball?"

"Yeah."

"Get it."

I take a baseball out of my bag. The Pitcher holds up an old baseball and looks at me with lined red eyes.

"You gotta always have a baseball. You gotta make your hands strong. You gotta get used to always having a ball in your hand all the time," he says, talking to the old ball.

I look at him.

"Was that yours when you were a kid?"

He snorts. "It ain't that old! But ya gotta get used to carrying a ball with you all the time. You gotta be able to move your hand so the batter won't see it." The Pitcher moves the ball like it's alive. "Ya gotta be able to change to a two-seam or a four-seam fastball in a second and not let anybody see what you're doing." He takes out his Skoal and hunks tobacco into his lip. "It's your job to strike out the guy at the plate. He's getting paid to hit and you're getting paid to strike him out."

I move the ball in my hand and drop it.

"That's why you gotta start carrying the ball," he says, nodding. "You gotta make your wrist and fingers strong. You gotta start now or you'll never carry it with you. Pitching is about habits. You gotta get good habits. The rockheads have lousy habits."

"You say 'gotta' a lot."

He frowns.

"I say a lot of goddamn things. But you gotta listen and not tell me 'I say gotta a lot.' "

"OK."

The Pitcher reaches into a blue cooler and pulls out a Good Times.

"Another thing is ..." He cracks open the beer and upends the can, "... don't listen to anybody. When you are on the mound it is *you*. I had coaches always telling me what to pitch and they'd say, hey Jack, how come you didn't throw that curve? And I'd say, aww, you know, coach, I didn't see the signal." He tips his can toward me. "They knew I was lying, but I figure they are going to hang me anyway if we lose, so I might as well pitch what the hell I want."

"Yeah. OK."

The Pitcher shuts one eye. "You especially don't listen to some rockhead in the stands. Like that guy the other night who called you a wetback. You wanted to kill him, didn't you?"

"Yeah," I mutter, feeling my face warm.

"And your Mom almost did. But you can't let a guy mess up your head like that." He burps. "Don't you think I been called everything from a bum to a pervert by some loudmouth who don't know shit from shinola about baseball? I been called everything and worse by every rockhead son of a bitch there ever was. But here is the thing," he continues, waving his can. "You don't *ever* let them get to you. And if they do get to you, you *never* show it. Your mom can go stomp on that guy's foot, but you can't," he says, pumping his finger. "You gotta pitch and I don't care if they call you wetback or greaser or taco eater ... you gotta stay cool and do your job. You got it?"

"Yeah," I answer, meeting his eyes.

"Alright," he says, nodding. "Now let's see you move that ball around."

I move the ball in my fingers and drop it again in the dust. The Pitcher scratches his cheek and crooks a finger at the ground. "Pick it up. You gotta to do that every day, every hour, every minute. When I was your age I always had a baseball in my hand. I took it to the bathroom, to restaurants, to the Army ... I took it everywhere."

The Pitcher sets his beer on the bench, then pulls out a dirty white bucket. It's full of sand-colored rocks of different sizes and shapes. The rocks rumble up to the top and the Pitcher pulls one out from the center. He grabs the bucket and his beer and starts walking to the outfield like a man going to work. He stops and turns.

"You coming or what?"

"Oh ... yeah," I mumble, jumping up.

I follow him to the far side of the field where he sets the pail down.

"Damn, that's heavy," he mutters. The Pitcher fingers up a cigarette, then nods in the morning sun, clapping his lighter down. "Now ... let me see you hit that gull."

I frown and stare at him. "What?"

He points across the field.

"Go ahead. Let me see you hit that goddamn gull."

I stare at the gull on the field.

"Well ... what the hell are you waiting for?"

I turn to him. "Mom would kill me if I hit a gull with a rock.'"

The Pitcher snorts and shakes his head.

"Go ahead. You ain't going to hurt him, because you can't hit him."

I hesitate, then reach into the bucket and pull out a flat rock. I hold the rock in my hand and stare at the gull. I move the rock around and get a two-finger grip.

"Go ahead," he says. "That gull is perfectly safe with you throwing."

I move the rock again, shut one eye and draw back. The gull stays on one leg and doesn't move. I had thrown high. The Pitcher shakes his head.

"Don't ever throw sidearm. Guys who can't pitch throw sidearm."

I pick up another rock and throw it ten feet over the gull.

"Do it again."

I pick out another rock and it flies high and to the right. I know there is no way I am going to hit that gull. The Pitcher drinks his beer and says, "Do it again." I throw and throw and throw rocks until my arm feels like it is going to fall off. I go through half the bucket of rocks, then turn to him, hot and sore, and irritated.

"I can't hit the gull," I admit.

His grey eyes narrow in.

"Yeah ... well shut up and throw again."

I get down to these little rocks that go nowhere. The Pitcher makes me throw every rock, including some pebbles. I hate throwing the rocks already. He nods to me.

"Your arm hurt?"

"Yeah. It does."

"That's because you keep trying to throw the rock into the next state." He pokes his cigarette in the air. "An arm is worthless without a pilot and you don't got no pilot."

"It's impossible to hit that stupid gull."

The Pitcher stares at me.

"Are you kidding me?" he cries out. "Anybody could hit that gull. My *grandmother* could hit that goddamn gull, and she's dead!"

"Well I can't."

The Pitcher puts the cigarette in his mouth and picks up a rock.

"Watch, rockhead," he mutters. He looks like the picture in his garage with his leg kicked up. The rock wings through the air and drills the gull with an explosion of feathers.

"He's dead," I shout, watching the gull fall over.

"No, he ain't," the Pitcher replies. "He's just stunned."

Sure enough, the gull pops up and flies away.

"How'd you know that gull wasn't dead?"

The Pitcher crunches his beer can.

"Cuz I know how to pitch."

He hands me the empty bucket.

"Now go get the rocks."

13

PITCHER BILLY WAGNER WAS BORN right-handed and taught himself to pitch left. He broke his right arm twice when he was young and had no choice. He played in the majors and became a closer with a one-hundred-and-one-mile-an-hour fastball. I thought about Billy Wagner because the Pitcher hit that gull with his right arm. I mean, he's a southpaw and pitched lefty all twenty-five years in the majors. Maybe I was mistaken, but every time I think about him hitting that gull, I see him throwing with his right arm.

Anyway, I throw rocks all that first day. I hate those spinning rocks shooting out under the sun and landing everywhere but where he wants. He tells me to hit a tree. Hit home plate, hit second base, hit third base, throw one in the dugout, throw one at the backstop post. With a funny expression, he watches my squadron of rocks go flying. I won't say it is a pleasurable expression, more like somebody remembering something. He smokes and watches me throw in the blazing heat that is Florida.

Heat doesn't seem to bother him. He never takes a drink of water that I see. He just keeps drinking Good Times beer like an athlete in training. He never gets drunk. He just watches me, making adjustments, telling me to follow through. I start cussing and he asks if my mom lets me talk that way.

"Sometimes."

"Well don't do it around me. I got delicate ears. Now go pick up the goddamn rocks."

After every bucket, I have to go pick up the rocks in the hot sun. Then I finish the day jogging around the field four more times and doing sit-ups and push-ups. I told you, I really hate running and I'm pretty bad at it. I'm slow and I breathe like I'm about to die. I suck in the hot-baked grass that is suffocating. When I finish, I am bent over, holding onto my knees, feeling like I am going to pass out. It has to be like a hundred.

The Pitcher stands up and nods.

"That's enough for today," he says, and picks up his cooler of Good Times.

The second day he has on his Orioles hat and his old cleats. He smokes with his legs crossed, slumped down with one hand on his cheek like this Norman Rockwell print Mom taped to my door. The Pitcher stares out at the infield. I think maybe he is seeing the World Series, throwing that final foul tip his catcher grabbed. Or maybe he is just seeing the sand swirling around in the morning. Maybe he is just bored.

I hear a rumbling motor and I turn to the far parking lot. Fernando pulls up, then leans back on his Harley with his feet on the high pegs. He must have gone to the house and somehow got it out of Mom. I didn't tell you this, but Fernando used to pitch in high school and Mom says he was pretty good. I find it hard to believe Fernando was good at anything, man.

The Pitcher stands up.

"Grab the rocks."

I am tired of throwing rocks. They are tearing up my hand and my shoulder hurts. And they are heavy. I grab the bucket and lug the rocks across the field like someone about to fall over. The Pitcher sets his beer down and points to this skinny pine tree.

"Throw at the knothole in that tree," he says.

I put the rocks down and stare at the tree. Man, it looks a million miles away. It's like a Charlie Brown tree, you know, the little Christmas tree in the cartoon. There is no way I can hit the tree with a rock. And it is impossible to hit the knothole because I can't even see it!

"I don't see any knothole."

"Don't be a rockhead." He points with his cigarette again. "It's right there."

I squint and see this faint circle the size of an egg.

"You want me to hit *that* with a rock?"

"Yeah. You got a problem with that?"

I stare at the tree, feeling sweat cooling all over my body. It is only nine o'clock and it is already ninety. I breathe heavily and I really want to learn how to pitch. I feel like that boy in the movie *Karate Kid* where the guy is teaching the boy how to wax his car you know, *wax on, wax off*. I mean that's cool, but I need to start *pitching*. The tryouts are coming up and I feel like I am getting worse.

So I turn to him and ask the question.

"We ever going to use baseballs?"

The Pitcher puts the cigarette to his mouth and shrugs.

"Baseballs are for people who know what they are doing. Rocks are for people who don't." He jabs a big finger at the bucket. "So pick up a rock and hit that knothole, rockhead."

I reach down and pick out a rock, mumbling, "I know how to throw a baseball."

"No you don't. You can't even throw a goddamn rock."

I hate it when people tell me I can't do something. It makes me see red, man. I stare at the tree on the edge of the field. Just hitting the trunk would be hard at this distance and hitting the knothole is impossible. I reach down and scoop up a flat rock.

"What are you doing?"

"Getting a different stupid rock," I grumble, hunting for a heavier one.

"Hey, *rockhead!*"

I stand and he points his cigarette at me.

"You know what you just told me?"

"No!"

"You just told me you *can't* hit that knothole! When you pitch to me, I'm going to knock it out of the park like I did to Bob Mariano in the series. When someone hits off you, I don't care if they blast it clear out of Wrigley Field into the lake! You don't show *nothing!* You got it rockhead? You throw the next pitch like you are the king of the world. You got that?"

"Yeah," I mutter, squinting up. "Why do you keep calling me rockhead?"

"Because until you learn to pitch, that's what you are."

Then something kind of bad happens. My phone is going off in my pocket. I have that Eminem tune *Lose Yourself* as my ringtone. Eminem keeps rapping away. *You only have one chance ...so don't blow it ...feet don't fail me now.*

I finally get my phone out and look up.

"What?"

"Give it to me," he says with his hand out.

The Pitcher keeps his hand out with these tough old-dog callouses, man. I give it to him. He leans back and *pitches* my phone across the field. My phone flies halfway to the infield and explodes. I can't even breathe, man. I mean that is my *lifeline* to the world and he just, he just ... *pitched it!*

"What the hell, man!" I cry out, staring at him.

"Yeah. I thought it would have gone further. I must be

getting old."

"You threw my phone!"

"Those things are pretty cheap, huh?" He frowns. "Must not be built in America."

"You ... you threw my phone!"

The Pitcher rolls his shoulders.

"You want to go talk on it then go get it. I'll get in my car and go home then."

"You just ..." I stare at him. "You just *destroyed* my phone!"

He levels his cigarette at me.

"Does a phone have anything to do with pitching? Is that thing going to give you control, going to give you a curve, or a sinker, or keep you from hitting the goddamn backstop?"

"No ... but—"

"That phone going to get you to hit that knothole?"

"No."

"Then shut up and start throwing the rocks."

The Pitcher cracks a beer and looks at me. I consider walking off. I really do.

"Yeah? ... You waiting for something?"

I kick the ground.

"No," I mutter, picking up another rock.

***

My thing is, I don't like to work. Not every day. And that's what we do. Every day we work at throwing rocks. He just watches me stand there like a soldier on the mound, blasting in these rocks across home plate. Or he sits on the bench sometimes while I go through the whole bucket. Then he motions his cigarette. "Go get 'em." Then I walk across that hot dusty infield to pick up the rocks.

But then one day he sits on the dugout bench and doesn't say a word.

"I finished," I tell him, sweating and hot.

The Pitcher's eyes hold the heat light, looking beyond me. He does that sometimes. He looks right over my head like he is seeing something else. And he doesn't move, his eyes going out to that dusty infield. He just sits there with his hands on the bench in the heat. I turn around and see he is staring at the pitcher's mound. And then he turns to me. He begins to open his mouth, then just shakes his head.

About the second week Mom comes across the field at noon. She walks up in a red dress with a flower in her hair. She's carrying a picnic basket. She spreads out a blanket and pulls out tortillas, guacamole, chips, fajitas, tacos. We eat our lunch and the Pitcher takes off his hat and smooths his hair and doesn't spit tobacco juice. He listens as Mom chatters on about the weather, the price of food, and then baseball.

"I have to pay you something for your help," she says, looking at him.

"No you don't."

Mom holds out the tube of twenties like an offering.

"Please take this. It will make me feel better," she continues, holding the rolled money with the rubber band around the middle.

The Pitcher shakes his head.

"I ain't taking your money."

Mom holds the money down, fingering the rubber band. "Then you have to let me do something," she says, pulling back her hair, her dark eyes catching the morning sun. "I can't take charity, Mr. Langford. I have to feel like I am doing something for you too."

He shuts one eye and rolls his shoulders.

"Well ... those fajitas you fixed the other night were pretty good."

"Then you come over and I'll make you a dinner."

The Pitcher waves his hand through the air.

"You don't gotta."

"It will make me feel better," she insists, rubbing a callous on her hand from playing ball. "I need to feel like I can pay you back some way." Mom stares at him, holding back her curly dark hair. "You get that, right?"

The Pitcher shrugs.

"Yeah, sure. A home-cooked meal."

She puts the money back into her dress.

"How's tomorrow night then?"

"I got nothing going on."

Mom smiles again. She really doesn't want to feel like we are taking charity. Even in our worst times she won't take food stamps or anything like that. But I also know she is making sure the Pitcher hangs in there with the Mexican kid with his crazy arm.

'Cause my arm *is* crazy, man.

14

MOM IS STIRRING RICE AND warming some taco shells while I put on this white shirt I wore to church and never wore again except for a wedding. I slip on long pants and brush my hair and button my shirt to the top. Then I help Mom set the table and she puts flowers in the middle. We look at each other when the doorbell rings.

"Go answer the door, Ricky," she says, smoothing her curly hair, looking in the mirror of the microwave, touching her lipstick.

Mom looks great with her jangling earrings. She looks like one of those women on television getting a diamond ring in a restaurant. I'd like to give Mom a diamond ring, because she sold hers a long time ago. I smooth down my hair, which is short anyway.

The Pitcher is standing there and he doesn't look normal. He drops his cigarette and nods when I open the door. He has on a blue sport coat over his golf shirt and khaki pants and is wearing loafers.

He looks more like a salesman than an MLB pitcher who won a World Series. He just doesn't look right without his ratty old shorts.

"Come in," I say, nervous as hell.

The Pitcher follows me while my heart goes *rumbdadum*.

We eat on the patio. The stars are bright and a moon hovers over the fence. The Pitcher has three tacos and two plates of rice and two margaritas. The candles flicker and the Pitcher doesn't say much. I can't think of anything to say but Mom just keeps chattering. I kind of zone out and then somehow Mom is talking about immigration and the Pitcher says you can't just let people come here illegally. Her eyes flare and I pray she won't start giving him the attitude. She leans into the candles.

"You think we should deport all those people, Mr. Langford?"

He raises his eyebrows, creaking his chair.

"You gotta send them back. What's fair is fair. Like you people. Wouldn't be fair to you after you went through the trouble becoming citizens."

Mom pulls her hair back behind her ear.

"But what if they have created lives here with families and jobs?"

The Pitcher shakes out a cigarette.

"They gotta go," he says, looking up at her.

I see Mom pause, then she stands and starts clearing the table. I know how hard it is for her not to tell him where to get off, but she just smiles tightly and takes away his plate and grabs mine. No one says much after that. The Pitcher yawns and looks like a statue. I keep seeing that picture where he jumped into the arms of his catcher and won the Word Series. I look down and will my mouth to open.

"What ..." I start again while he stares at the Mexican kid dribbling into his plate. I give myself a count, timing it to the drumbeat of my heart. *One, two, three!*

"What was it like to pitch in the World Series?"

The Pitcher puts his lighter on the table. He leans back and holds the cigarette down to his side. His eyes come down from the sky and center on me.

"It was great," he says simply.

Mom walks out and he stands up and holds her chair, then scoots it in. I noticed earlier the Pitcher let her walk ahead of him and held the patio door open. Now, he fills her wine glass and lights her cigarette before he sits back down.

"Thanks for dinner."

Mom smiles.

"It's the least I can do."

Then we sit on the back patio and Mr. Hallapene from next door comes out. He wears those old guy T-shirts that hang down, with his skinny arms sticking out. Mom says he was in the war and I'm not sure which one, but he has all these blue tattoos on his arms. He stays outside in his garden watering his plants or something, then turns on his radio and this Cuban music floats over like in one of those old-time movies.

"That's the tango," Mom says, nodding.

The Pitcher ashes his cigarette and shakes his head.

"That's a dance I always thought would be kind of fun," he says, pausing. "My wife wanted us to learn ... but we never did."

Mom jumps up.

"Come on, I'll show you."

The Pitcher stares at her like she just stripped or something.

"That's not for me."

"Bullshit," Mom says, pulling him up.

And I mean he is one big dude and Mom uses everything to get him on his feet. The Pitcher stands there awkwardly with his big hands hanging down. Mom moves his hands around like a mannequin.

"Alright, put your one hand on my waist," she says, putting it around her waist. "And raise your other and I hang on to it like this."

I can tell the Pitcher isn't used to this. He's not used to

anybody telling him what to do, but Mom is perfect at that. She looks up at him and smiles.

"Are you ready, Mr. Langford?"

"I don't know."

Mr. Hallapene's music is really going now.

"You can do this," she says, real small next to him. "Ready ... one, two, three!"

And they step across our small patio and then Mom says, "OK, now turn and back." And the Pitcher and Mom turn and they step back to the table and then go away again. "Now dip me," she commands after they go back and forth three times. The Pitcher dips Mom and her hair flies down. They stay like that for a moment and then he brings her up.

"That was fun," she says, smoothing back her hair.

"Yeah, it was."

Mom smiles and taps him lightly on the shoulder.

"I told you you could do it," she whispers. "See ... you are a very good dancer, Mr. Langford."

The Pitcher has these two spots of red on his cheeks.

"That was really fun," he says, holding the chair for Mom.

I know how he's feeling. Mom has a way of getting you to do what you think you never could. I guess even MLB pitchers need a kick sometimes.

Suddenly it's like I'm not even there. I mean it's kind of weird, because Mom becomes this other person and laughs and smiles teasingly. She flips her hair and her earrings jangle. I smell her perfume on the breeze. The candlelight plays on her cheeks as she tells the Pitcher about moving from Chicago. I ride the tide, man.

"Your ex-husband?"

"Ex-asshole," Mom corrects him. " Fernando was the reason we moved out here. He hated the winters in Chicago."

"Yeah. I don't care for the white stuff either," the Pitcher agrees, shaking his head.

Mom rubs the stem of her wine glass. Her mouth pinches in and her voice lowers.

"I wanted to thank you for that night ...," she begins, meeting his eyes. "I appreciate what you did for Ricky and me."

The Pitcher frowns and shakes his head.

"Don't know what you mean."

I know his game. If he threw that ball at Fernando's motorcycle, he wouldn't admit it. It's like he doesn't want to be caught doing something nice. It's the pitcher code, which is you don't show anything. You keep your emotions down low.

"Well ... thank you anyway." Mom pauses, then looks at him. "I heard you have Ricky throwing rocks."

"Yeah." He smiles lightly. "He's thrown a few."

Mom tilts her head.

"Is that to develop his technique?"

"It's how I learned."

Mom nods and I can see she's probing, trying to make sure I'm going to learn to pitch from him. She stares at her cigarette. "If Ricky doesn't make the high school team, he probably won't play baseball again." She looks at him. "You saw him pitch. Don't you think he needs a change-up?"

"He don't need a change-up."

"But all he knows is how to pitch hard."

The Pitcher sits back and looks at Mom.

"Do you even know what a change-up is, Ms. Hernandez?"

Her eyes darken. "Yes ... it's a slower fastball."

"No. That ain't what a change-up is."

"Then why don't you *show* Ricky what it is?"

I hear the squeal of the patio door and Fernando busts out of the darkness like a pirate swinging onto a ship. His eyes are bright and he's sweating. He kicks the door closed and smiles, but it's not a good smile.

"Little perfect family here, huh?"

Mom turns around.

"What the hell do you want, Fernando?"

"Nothing baby," he says, shrugging. "Just stopping by, you know. You looking fine, Maria," he continues. "I ain't seen that dress in a long time, man. Last time I got laid I think." Fernando holds up his hand for a high-five. "What up, little man?" He stares at me and frowns. "You all dressed up too, bro? Trying to make the big impression, huh? "

"Yeah," I mutter, hitting his hand lightly.

"Damn!" He stares at the Pitcher, shaking his head. "You finally came out of your garage, huh? Let me shake your hand, dude!" Fernando grabs the Pitcher's hand. He stares at me and shakes his head *like damn, man, how about this?* "This is the real shit, man, a major league pitcher! Maria got all over you about coaching, Ricky, huh?"

The Pitcher shrugs.

"I just came over for dinner with my neighbors."

Fernando walks around the patio.

"Yeah, man. I bet she been thinking about you a long time." He leans on the table, lowering his voice. "So tell me bro ... you think my son has an arm?"

The Pitcher doesn't move. It is *the question* and it's weird that Fernando asked it. The Pitcher looks up at Fernando and takes out his Marlboros.

"Yeah ..." He nods. "I think he does."

Fernando flips around a chair and sits down, leaning forward with his tattoos bulging.

"You know, I was over here the other night. And somebody threw a baseball, man, and broke the windshield to my Harley." He leans back and stares at the Pitcher. "You know anything about that?"

The Pitcher puffs up a cigarette.

"Maybe a bird flew into it," he replies.

Fernando stares at him, then smiles slowly.

"Yeah man, that's right." He laughs. " A motherf------ bird

hit it."

"I wouldn't know," he says, clapping his lighter shut.

"Right, man. Right." Fernando nods slowly. "You wouldn't know. You're just the weird dude across the street that used to be an MLB pitcher, right?" He turns to Mom, speaking in a low voice. "And now Maria has her whore dress on with her son all pimped up to be the perfect Mexican family, right?"

Mom points toward the street.

"Get the hell out of here!"

He shakes his head.

"Oh, baby. I just got here. I don't want to blow it for you, man, but since I worked with Ricky and developed his arm, I figure I have some say, you know."

"You never worked with me," I mutter, surprising myself.

Fernando stares at me, his eyes narrowing. My heart is pounding, but I know how Fernando rolls. He wants to take all the credit for anything good. He wants to take credit for something Mom did.

"Oh I get it, bro," he nods slowly. "Yeah, you the man now, huh?" He gets in my face, his whiskey breath like gasoline. "Figure you got your game on now and your little arm, and you can say anything to your dad who worked his ass off with you on your pitching!"

I don't know. I should just roll with it, but I can't take Fernando saying *he* worked on my pitching. So I give him my death stare, you know, and say real loud, "You never did anything with me!"

My heart is jacking up and down, because Fernando looks like he wants to kill me. He leans closer and I can feel him breathing like a dog about to bite.

"What'd you say, you little shit?"

I meet his dark glittery eyes. My heart is about out of my chest. *Boom Boom Boom.*

"I said ... you never worked with me ... Mom did!"

Fernando backs up and nods with this weird little smile.

"Sure, man. Right. You figure you get yourself an MLB coach, man, and you go all the way, huh?" He shakes his head. "Forget about your Mom who was a *f------ loser* when I met her."

"You're the loser!" I shout.

Fernando jumps up and grabs me by the collar. My feet leave the ground and he starts spitting his whiskey breath all over me.

"Oh you the big man now, huh?! Think you got something over me? I'll kick your motherf------ ass!"

Then he falls and I hit the patio. I look up and the Pitcher is standing with his chair, holding it like a bat. Fernando is on his knees and coughing. I mean our patio furniture is iron and heavy, but the Pitcher holds the chair like it's nothing. Fernando stands, grabbing his back and staring at him.

"You're dead," Fernando croaks.

"Anytime, rockhead," the Pitcher says coolly.

Mom grabs her purse and whips out the rolled hundred bucks. It's like the money no one will take, but I know Fernando will take it.

"*Here!*" She shoves the money in his hand. "Take it and get out, asshole!"

Fernando holds the money, then puts it in his pocket.

"Yeah, man," he growls, glaring at Mom. "He's going to blame your dumb Mexican ass when he finds out he's just like everybody else."

He looks at the Pitcher.

"I'll see you again, *cabrón.*"

And then Fernando kicks back the patio door. I don't breathe until I hear his Harley rumble alive and whine down the street. Then it is just quiet. Mom is standing there like she has a terrible headache. Our little table with the candles looks like a crime scene. Mom looks at the Pitcher.

"I am so sorry ..."

He has his hands on the back of the chair. She just trails

off, because really, there is nothing to say. We are just the poor dumbass Mexican family to him now. There is no way he's going to coach me. Everything we had worked for just crashed. It's like one of those bad ESPN dinners where the player walks off and never comes back.

The Pitcher looks down.

"Listen ..." He pauses and I don't like the feeling. "I was going to tell you and the boy earlier ... something has come up and I have other commitments now. I figured I'd wait until you made me dinner to tell you. So now you don't feel you owe me anything for the lessons."

He says it like he just put the last brick in a wall. I feel like someone has just pulled my chair out from under me. I want to go back to when they were doing the tango and everything was good. Mom sits back in her chair and looks at him.

"Your commitments just came up?"

"Yeah," he says, looking at the table.

And we can both tell he is lying. It is like he just shut down or something. But I know what it is. He figures drinking beer in his garage is better than being in a hot field with some Mexican kid with a psycho dad. But I feel bad, man. It's like being cut from a team. It's like being cut from my dream. But Mom ... she's pissed.

"So you are just going *to quit* on him?"

The Pitcher frowns and shifts his legs.

"I wouldn't put it like that."

"Really?' Mom stares at him, her eyes snapping. "You are quitting on a boy when he needs you most and you don't call that quitting?"

The Pitcher breathes heavily .

"*Ms.* ..."

"Hernandez ... Call me Maria."

"Maria ... I don't mind giving your son my time for the last few weeks," he begins. "But I'm really not a coach. Hell, I don't even coach men anymore who pay five grand to pretend that they are a major leaguer and wear a uniform and run around a diamond."

"I'm not talking about men in *fantasy camps*," Mom snaps. "I am talking about my son, who has a chance to play on the high school team! He has a dream and he has a gift. And I'm going to do everything in my power to see that he gets his dream."

The Pitcher shrugs.

"If he works at it he might get some control. But he has some basic problems that I—"

"Of course he has *problems*," Mom nearly screams. "That's why he can't control the ball!"

The Pitcher shakes his head.

"Listen, I was a pitcher. I was never a coach and the problems he has are going to take a lot more time to solve than I have."

"Oh, I see," Mom says, nodding. "So you quit because you can't just show him some pitches and have him perform them perfectly?"

"That ain't it—"

"It's alright, Mom," I blurt out. "It's alright. I'll be fine." I really want her to quit begging. "I learned some stuff I can use," I say, shrugging.

Mom just stares at me because she knows I'm lying.

"The tryouts are a month away," she says to the Pitcher.

He doesn't speak for a moment.

"Thanks for the dinner," he says quietly, then starts toward the gate.

It's the high school team walking away under the moon. Baseball is going to end on this patio on this night. Then Mom starts crying. I mean sniffling and wiping her eyes. She just can't help it. The Pitcher reaches the gate and stops.

"Look ... if you work with him and he remembers some of the things—"

"Bullshit," Mom says, her voice breaking. "I'm not a pitcher!"

I see his back raise up and I hear his breath.

"Shit," he mutters.

He turns around slowly and looks at Mom.

"A change-up, Ms. Hernandez ..."

Mom wipes her eyes and looks at him.

"... is the difference between what's expected and what actually happens."

The Pitcher pauses, then looks at me.

"Eight o'clock at the field. Don't be late."

Then he just pushes open the patio door and walks off.

PITCHING IS NOT A NATURAL act. Pitching requires your arm and shoulder to go to a point where they will break down. You ever watch a guy like Bobby Jenks pitch a one-hundred-and-one fastball? You watch him and *you know* what pitching is all about. I think about that while I throw those rocks, because I feel like my arm is about to blow apart. I manage to hit the tree a few times and even start to get a rhythm where I hear the rock hit the wood. I throw rocks for three more days and then the Pitcher shows up with his mitt.

I pick up the blackened glove and put my nose into the leather.

"You use this when you pitched in the World Series?"

"Of course I did," he grumbles, pulling out the bucket. "You ready?"

I set down the mitt and look at the bucket. My heart sinks.

"More rocks?" I groan.

The Pitcher pulls off the lid to a bucket of ... baseballs.

"You got a problem with that?"

"No!"

"Then toss me my glove, rockhead."

I throw him his mitt.

"Now, let's just play catch," he says. "Just nice and easy. No hauling it to the moon."

He tosses me a baseball and I toss it back. I feel like singing. The sun is shining and we are throwing a *baseball!* I whip the ball back to him and he tosses it back nice and easy.

"Alright, take a step back."

I step back. The ball sails from the Pitcher, smooth and straight like a train in the air. I try to make mine smooth and straight, but he has to reach for it.

"What the hell did I just tell you?"

"What?"

"Just *throw* the goddamn ball," he commands. "You gotta learn to just throw. Just throw the ball."

"I am!"

"No. You ain't. You're throwing it like *you think* you should, like you think the way you're supposed to pitch. Forget about pitching. You ain't a pitcher yet. You just gotta throw the ball, you got it?"

"Yeah," I mutter, throwing the ball back.

"There." He nods. "You didn't think about it. Now take another step back."

We keep throwing and stepping back until we are at opposite ends of the field. The Pitcher throws the ball like a rocket launched from his shoulder. The ball sails out from him like he was doing nothing. I have to throw with everything I have just to reach him. We throw for what seems like a half-hour, then we meet in the middle of the field.

"Your arm hurt, rockhead?"

"Yeah," I say, shrugging. "A little."

It hurts *a lot,* from my shoulder on down, but I'm not going to tell him. To me this is my school. This is my ticket to the freshman high school team and I don't care if my arm falls off. The Pitcher stuffs Skoal in his lip and spits.

"Your arm hurts because you're still pitching like a rockhead. You are trying too hard and overstraining your arm. Look..." He holds the baseball in front of him. "You need to just throw it. You believe that if you strain harder it will make it go faster. That ain't true. You just have to throw the ball. You are thinking about it way too much. Forget everything you think you know about pitching. Just do what you did with the rocks."

"What's that?"

"Don't think. You overthink every goddamn thing. Just throw the goddamn ball."

"You think you could show me a change-up sometime?"

"You don't need no change-up. I never needed one and neither do you."

"Yeah but ... if they see my fastball then ..."

"Hey, *rockhead*." He rifles the dust with Skoal. "You pinch the corners. You throw one by their chin at ninety miles an hour. Show them who's boss. You won't need no change-up," he says, holding his cigarette to his mouth. "You just worry about throwing strikes, alright?"

"Yeah alright."

"Besides, you gotta throw a lot of crappy balls before you can throw a strike and you throw a lot of crappy balls."

I squint up at him.

"I guess major league pitchers started this way, huh?"

The Pitcher spits another long brown steak of tobacco juice.

"Those rockheads don't know how to pitch."

16

HEY, I'M GOING TO TELL you about minor league baseball. Minor league teams can be Single A, Double A or Triple A. Triple A is the best and single A is usually for the rookies. The whole minor league thing is called the farm system. Guys play on these teams a few years and either get bumped up to another level or to the majors, or that's it. It's also where major leaguers are sent for rehab or if they're not needed. In Triple A you see guys on their way to the majors and guys on their way down from the majors. What's coolest is the guys who are trying to make it. The pitchers sit in folding chairs on the side of the field and wait their turn to pitch. They all have on their clean white uniforms and it's like they are soldiers, waiting to go to war.

Mom and I once saw the Florida Badgers, an AA minor league team, for ten bucks in Badger Stadium. It's a pretty cool stadium, built next to a landfill. Sometimes it smells like garbage, but most nights the wind is going the other way. Anyway, here's the deal: Today, we are having our game in the same place! I feel my breath leave when I see the diamond with the perfect grass and the infield with no rocks or divots or holes. This is the scene in the movie where the team plays the tournament champs and high school coaches are observing the game.

Which will be the case!

Mom and I walk around the field before the game and stare at the empty stands. It is like we are in a coliseum or something. You can just imagine all those people watching you. The lights are on and I feel like I am straight up big leagues. The baselines are like the lines of the highway and the batter's box is a perfect square. Everything about the place is majors, and me and everybody else think about being here for real one day.

Then the game starts.

The announcer's voice shoots our names into space, man. That's how it sounds with voices echoing all over the place as they announce players coming to bat and rock music plays between innings. Everyone immediately begins to play up. You play a good team, or play in a really cool stadium, and you play better than you ever did before. We battle neck and neck with the Ft. Meyers Dusters through the first five innings until we pull away and score off a double. Then a triple. Suddenly the Dusters are chasing two.

Then in the bottom of the sixth, Artie Ravioli digs a grave with three walks. Artie just can't throw a strike and the Dusters coach give their batters the take sign. They just stand there and don't swing and get on base with walks. I know how Artie feels. The worst feeling is when you can't find the zone and the other team knows it. So we watch Artie die out there in the middle of Badger Stadium. That's when Mom walks up to Devin by the fence.

"They're all getting the take sign."

He is working the gum in his cheek like it is on fire.

"Yeah, maybe I should get Eric back in there," he mutters.

"But he already pitched!"

Devin turns, his mirrored sunglasses reflecting the field.

"We need to get out of this inning, Maria."

Just then the batter cracks one deep in left field. We watch as two runners rotate in and we are tied.

"Devin, we need to make a change," Mom says again, shaking her head.

If it wasn't for Mom, Devin could give Eric all the pitching time he wants. Mrs. Payne videotaped Devin and Eric on the mound before the game. I'm sure to them this was the future where they pose with their *major league* son.

"All the boys deserve a chance to pitch in the stadium," Mom insists, pulling up her sunglasses on her hat.

"Hey. This isn't *kindergarten* where everyone gets a chance," he snaps. "This is baseball and the best players have to be fielded!"

"Oh and that just happens to be *your* son?"

"At least I don't have to dig up some old pitcher to give my kid an edge."

"No, you send your kid to every Finish First camp you can find!"

Devin breathes heavily and stares out at the field where Artie is dying. He grips the mesh of the dugout and lowers his head. "Alright ... I might need Eric in tomorrow's game ..." He turns to me, snapping out the words. "Get warmed up, Ricky. I need you to close it down for us."

"Sure thing, coach," I say, jumping up.

Mom winks. I know she wants me to pitch on that minor league mound in Badger Stadium. I mean, usually our fields are washed out mud pits of hard clay and grass that look like they've been burned over. But a real ball field is amazing and it can make all sorts of things happen. Like that movie *Field of Dreams*, right? It was kind of a weird movie, but baseball fields are magical.

All you want to do is play on them.

***

So I'm on the mound in Badger Stadium and there' s a warm breeze blowing in. It's one of the most perfect moments of my life—except I have loaded the bases and we are down by one. The seats surround the field like a cozy old house. The infield is dark green and the baselines are pure white. It would be really cool if I wasn't losing the game for us. I keep trying to remember something the Pitcher has taught me. *Push off your back leg. Use the rubber. Don't step off sideways. Point your shoulder. Follow through. Tuck your glove. Pitch like you are hitting a man. Pick a spot.* None of it is working.

So I am not surprised to see Mom walking out to the mound. She walks out under the dusty halo of light with her hair curling out the back of her cap. I see a defeated kid in her glasses. He's looking down and doesn't look at all like a pitcher to me.

"How are you doing there, champ?"

"I think I'm going to lose the game for us."

"Bullshit," she says. "What has Mr. Langford been telling you?"

"We've mostly been throwing rocks. We just started using baseballs."

Mom pulls up her glasses and rubs her forehead.

"Alright, listen. Take your breath and concentrate. Just try and remember something he told you. Did he tell you anything, Ricky ... anything that could help you? What about a change-up?"

"He doesn't believe in them."

Mom breathes heavily, then puts her hands on my shoulders.

"Look at me, Ricky. Pitch him your fastball. If you throw the way you know how, then you will have him. Just relax and take your breath."

"Yeah. OK, Mom."

"OK." She holds up her fist. "Now do it, Carlos!"

She gives me a knuckle bump and walks away. I stare at the batter who has already pegged one out of the park that went foul. He's big and swings the bat like he's going to kill the ball. He nods like he's saying, *I'm going to blast it down your throat.* I take a deep breath and pull on the brim of my hat. Eric moves his mitt low.

I shake off his signals.

"C'mon, let's finish the game!"

"He's done!"

I glance at our dugout and see Mom hold her hand to her chest. *Take your breath.* I pull my hands in and position my fingers between the seams. *Pick a spot, pick a spot.* I pick Eric's outside knee. I breathe deeply, tilting my head low. I stare at the batter who thinks I'm the Mexican kid who can't hit the corners. He figures he'll plant this one over the fence. I figure he will too.

I breathe one more time, say a quick prayer, then break my hands, pushing off the rubber and keeping my body square. Then I follow through like I'm punching someone. He fouls off right. I try the same pitch again and he fouls off left. Eric is staring at me because all the wildness is gone and I'm *placing* the ball. The batter is beating home plate. He's mad now. I try a change-up and throw a blooper over his head. Eric scurries to the backstop to get it.

He turns and throws the ball and right away I know something is different. I hold the ball in my hand. It's too heavy. Baseballs left out in the rain soak up the water and become like cannon balls. We have some waterlogged balls we throw to the side and a couple have wedged under the backstop. I stare at Eric as he pounds his mitt.

I go into my set, holding the heavy ball. I take my breath, kick back, and throw that round weight with everything I have. It sails to the plate like a melon. The Ft. Meyers batter rears back and blasts that melon right out of the park. I turn and watch the ball arc over the back fence, becoming small. The players start rotating in on the grand slam and everyone spills out of their dugouts.

Eric throws me a new ball the umpire had given him.

I hold it in my hand. The ball is light as a feather.

17

YEAH, WALKING ACROSS THE STREET under the moon, I'm feeling sorry for myself. You do that when you blow a game in a minor league stadium with everyone watching. I came off that mound like a dog and when I asked Eric about the waterlogged ball, all he did was laugh.

"You can't blame me because all you got is a fastball, beano," he said, shaking his head.

And listening to the Pitcher's television coming from under his garage, I know he was right. All I still had was my fastball. I needed another pitch and that's why I slipped out while Mom watched *Dancing with the Stars*. I pause outside the garage and hear the television rambling on. It sounds like a talk show. Then Shortstop clicks over to the garage and I see his nose.

I kneel on the cement as he ducks out, tail wagging.

"Hey Shortstop, where's your dad? He asleep?"

I look under the garage, hesitate, then swing under and stand up. The television is loud and a blond-haired man faces me. *"You see in America, we demand people come here legally. These people have come here illegally and they should be sent back to where they come from. It is the right of Arizona to protect their own borders and no one can tell them they can't ... least of all the president."*

I see cigarettes in beer cans and hockey pucks of Skoal on the floor. I glance at the photo of the Pitcher jumping into his catcher's arms. I walk closer and nearly trip over the Pitcher. He's lying on his side on the cold concrete with one arm on his hip. I hunch down and stare at the empty bottle beside him. I'm back with Fernando on the living room floor smelling all fermented. He would binge and lay around the house groaning for two days. Mom said that's the way it rolls with some alcoholics. They binge and drink for like three days straight. Mom had to go get Fernando a lot of times at some bar or in some alley.

I stare at the Pitcher and the question starts there. I always thought Fernando drank because he didn't have a job. But here's this dude who pitched in *a World Series* and was *MVP* and had millions of people cheering him. He was on baseball cards and faced down the greats. He lived the dream, right? So why would he get drunk and pass out in his garage? I mean, when I was on the mound in Badger Stadium, it was like I was Leonardo DiCaprio on the deck of the Titanic or something. You know, *I'm on top of the world!* But Mom says everyone has troubles and money and fame don't change that.

So I watch the Pitcher snore for a moment, then I pick up the remote and find a ballgame: Sox and the Yankees in the third with the Sox up by two. I put the remote by his cigarettes on the floor and bring over his Skoal. I grab the torn beer can he uses for an ashtray, then take a blanket off the bed and drape it over him. I walk to the garage door and turn. The Pitcher is snoring on the floor under the ballgame. The crowd roars.

18

MOM DROPS ME OFF AT the field the next morning. There is no sign of the Pitcher and I sit down on the dugout bench engraved with *Johnny loves Joany*. At about nine o'clock I know something is wrong. I sit on the bench staring at the sunny infield, imagining myself on the mound pitching a no-hitter. Then I am throwing the final pitch of a World Series and jumping into the arms of my catcher. The world comes swarming out of the stands and I'm voted MVP for the series.

At ten o'clock I tell myself a lot of people can drink and still get up. I saw it with Fernando. Sometimes he was all drunked up, but went off to work anyway. So I hope the Pitcher is waiting until he has a few cigarettes and does the *hair of the dog* thing with a couple cans of Good Times. But it's now eleven o'clock.

When Mom dropped me off she said she didn't see his station wagon. I said maybe he came a different way and I looked away from her gaze. She knew something was up last night when I told her I didn't feel like watching ESPN. I had hit the sheets and made the room really dark. That's when I heard her knock.

"Yeah," I said from under my blankets.

"What happened with Mr. Langford, Ricky?"

"He was asleep," I murmured.

"Asleep?"

"Yeah. Asleep."

"You were over there all that time and he was *asleep?*"

"*Yeah.*"

Mom eventually left.

Now I'm having one of those moments where you know someone isn't coming. It happens sometimes when I hang around Target or Best Buy and a text comes back, *sorry bro, I forgot, catch up with you later.* I look across the field, willing an image of the Pitcher crossing with his bucket and cooler. He's smoking and spitting and drinking beer. But who I see is Mom and she's walking fast.

I sure hope the Pitcher put his garage all the way down this time.

"Where is he?"

That's the first thing she asks. Mom has come back with a cooler of Gatorade and water and PowerBars. Her eyes are rocking back and forth like he's hiding under the bench. She puts her hands on her hips and leans forward, pushing her sunglasses up in her hair. She lowers her chin and asks me again, "Where the hell is he?"

"He didn't show," I mumble.

"I can see that! Where the hell *is* he?"

I just keep my head down, turning the baseball in my mitt. I feel like somebody took that poster board in my room of Wrigley Field and crumpled it up. And that's probably why, you know, my eyes are kind of hot. Mom sits down next to me.

"What happened last night, Ricky?"

I roll my shoulders again. I do that when the eyes start up, because the voice goes at the same time. First of all, *dudes don't cry*. And if you do, you do it when *no one* is looking, especially your mom. But this thing was so heavy, I couldn't keep it away.

"I don't know," I mutter, wiping my eyes.

"Ricky! *Talk to me!*"

I breathe heavily, looking down at the dirt. I'm trying not to think about the Pitcher. I don't want to think he is lying in his garage on the floor. I didn't think pitchers were that way. They are disciplined. They always talk on television about how they can improve. They are winners. They don't pass out in their garage from drinking Jack Daniel's.

"What happened, Ricky?"

I roll my shoulders a couple of times.

"I went over there last night ..."

Mom leans close.

"And ..."

"... he was passed out on the floor of his garage."

Mom stares at me like she doesn't believe me. She sits back on the dugout bench and rubs the finger she used to wear her wedding ring on. There had been a light band of skin on her finger until the sun filled it in. Then she wore another ring that kind of looked like her old one. She said it was to keep the creeps away. The Pitcher had just become one of those creeps.

"What do you mean he was passed out on the floor?"

"I couldn't wake him up. I shook him and he didn't move," I mutter.

Mom blinks, her eyes turning into a jury.

"Shit." She rubs her eyes like she wants to tear them out. Mom stares across the field. "He had to be a goddamn drunk."

I look at her and for some reason I feel a little better.

"You want to throw it around some, Mom?"

She glares at me.

"*Am I* teaching you how to pitch, Ricky?"

"No ... but—"

"You don't need another playmate," she snaps. "You need

a coach!" Mom stands up. "I'm going to find this broken down bastard—"

"Don't say anything," I plead, really alarmed she will make things worse. "Don't say anything. *Please!*"

Mom stares at me. "He's not coming back tomorrow, Ricky! He's just like your father and I would think by now you know how that goes!"

"He is not Fernando, Mom!" I shout.

She leans forward like she's going to jump on me. I have seen her this way before with Fernando. Once Mom's lit, it's hard to put out the fire.

"And how do you know that? How do you know he isn't just like your father, Ricky? He is just like all men who are assholes!"

"Because ... he's not Mom. He just got drunk is all."

She breathes deeply and stares at the backstop.

"Well this is one drunk who is going to hear from me. "

And that's when I said something I shouldn't have. I mean I have Mom's temper if you haven't noticed and it gets me in trouble a lot.

"Mom," I say, staring at her. "You are going to screw everything up again by being a bitch!"

My arm nearly comes out when she grabs me. Mom is strong and when she's angry she's really strong. But I've gotten stronger too and I pull back against her. She lets me go and I fall back right on my butt. She shouts at me like a crazy woman.

"Don't you ever call me that word again! Do you understand?!"

I glare at her, but my eyes won't stop leaking. It's like we're both on fire now and we want to tear each other to pieces.

"Why?" I yell back. "You're just making things worse like you always do!"

And then she steps back and we stare at each other. I think neither of us wants things to get this out of control. Mom takes a step, then her eyes well up and I feel really bad for calling her a bitch. I try to apologize, but it's like she isn't there. She just wipes her eyes and speaks in a real cold voice.

"We are leaving. Please bring your equipment."

Then she turns and walks back across the field. I have never heard Mom speak like that before. She went from hot to cold in seconds. And Mom never calls anything *equipment*. So I grab my bat bag and follow her across the hot field.

Things can't get any worse.

But of course I am wrong.

19

TENNIS BALLS DON'T ACT LIKE baseballs. They are too light and smaller in your hand. But they don't break windows and put dents in garage doors. I hold the tennis ball in and take my breath, aiming for the third square from the bottom in our door. That is my spot. I kick back and see the batter I was going to fan with my inside fastball. I come over the top and follow through like I am punching a man. The tennis ball smacks the garage door and bounces high. I lunge and see Mom on the porch.

"Come on," she commands, walking across the street.

I groan because I know this is not going to be good. I follow Mom across the hot street and up his drive. I want to warn the Pitcher that a storm is coming his way. He really should have just left town for a few days. That's what you do in Florida when hurricanes roll in.

Mom marches up to the garage and whams on the door, shouting.

"Mr. Langford! I have to speak with you!"

Man, my heart is jumping now. Mom stands there with her hands on her hips like she's daring the whole world. Shortstop tilts his head, his ears perking, then lies back down. Dogs. Nothing riles them, man. Just sleep, sleep, sleep. I wouldn't mind being a dog sometimes.

Like now!

"Mr. Langford!" Mom shouts again, hitting the garage door. We wait and she looks at me.

"Maybe we should come back, Mom," I suggest.

The heat is coming up from the drive in hot oily waves. Florida is an oven and maybe Mom wonders for the hundredth time what she is doing here. We're stuck, like everyone else in the country that moved, right? Nobody is moving anywhere except into their cars or into shelters. And we might end up there too one day.

She pounds on the garage again.

"Mr. Langford!"

We listen and I can faintly hear his television. I figure this is going nowhere but bad. Mom has a head of steam up. I heard her on the phone talking in Spanish to Grandma. When she gets really pissed she talks in Spanish. I think that is so she can swear like crazy. But after she hung up, she seemed even madder.

"Mom ... let's just go," I whisper. "We can come back later."

"No!" She shakes her head. "I'm going to find this asshole." Then she looks at me and gestures to the cement. "Go under there and find him, Ricky."

I stare at her and touch my chest.

"What?"

"Go under the garage and tell me if he is in there," she orders.

"Mom, I really don't—"

"Go!"

I wiggle under the door and stand up in the dark garage. I inhale something really bad, like rotten food or when you get the stomach flu. My eyes adjust and I see the Pitcher with white cheesy puke all over his shirt.

I turn back to the door.

"Mom, he's here," I call back.

She leans down to the gap in the garage.

"Where?"

"On the floor!" I shout, gesturing to him. "He has this gross puke all over him."

I look around and find the remote control for the door. Day comes in like a wave with light rolling up the walls. The air flows in too and I can breathe again. Mom walks in and sees the Pitcher and shakes her head.

"Jesus mother of Joseph," she says softly, bending down. "Mr. Langford ... *Mr. Langford ...*"

Mom shakes him and he doesn't move.

"Ricky, grab that roll of paper towels," she tells me.

I walk over to the microwave and grab the roll. Mom then shouts, "MR. LANGFORD!"

The Pitcher sits up like in an old horror movie and blinks. He turns to Mom with drool running down his chin. "Ohhhh ... shit" he groans.

"Oh shit is right," Mom mutters, wiping him down, unrolling half of the paper towels to clean up the vomit on the floor. She finds a garbage bag and some more paper towels. "Go wet these inside the house, Ricky."

I stare at her, because going in the house is freaky.

"Mom I don't think I should go in there—"

"Go, Ricky!"

Mom is more freaky, so I cross the garage and go into his house. The smell is the sour scent of old garbage. It smells like *nobody* lives here. Dust coats everything and I can see a trail in the dust leading to the kitchen. I follow the trail and turn on the faucet in a super-dirty sink. Then I glance in the living room. It looks like a woman lives here: stems from flowers, doilies under the lamps, paintings of flowers. I see a picture of a woman with the Pitcher.

She is beautiful, man.

***

The Pitcher sits in his chair like a man at a cop station. His hands tremble, holding the beer to his mouth like someone who just found water in the desert. A baseball next to his cigarettes falls and rolls on the cement. I pick it up while Mom finishes cleaning up the floor. She leans back on his refrigerator, crossing her arms.

"How do you feel?"

The Pitcher squints against the light from the fluorescent tube.

"Been better." He frowns. "Must have fallen out of my chair."

"You could say that." Mom pauses, rolling her tongue across her lips. "So this is how major league pitchers end up?"

He looks up at her.

"You expected something different?"

"I don't know." Mom shrugs. "Living in a garage and passing out in your puke on the floor ... yeah, I figured someone who pitched in a World Series, they might have come a little further."

The Pitcher tosses his lighter on the table next to the baseball and shrugs.

"Nope," he says, holding the cigarette by his cheek. "This is the way it ends up."

The Pitcher ashes his cigarette and settles back into the La-Z-Boy. Mom stands up from the refrigerator and rolls out her hand.

"Look, if you want to live in your garage and get drunk and puke, that's your business."

"That's right, it is."

"But when it involves my kid, then it concerns me," she

continues, covering the crucifix on her shoulder she usually keeps hidden.

"Maybe I ain't your coach then."

Bam! Just like that. Like the time Jimmy punched me in the stomach and I couldn't breathe for a full minute. Mom looks at me and our eyes meet.

"Ricky, wait for me outside," she orders.

I go to the side of the garage where she can't see me.

"So you're going to leave him just like that? These tryouts are in two weeks!"

"He has an arm but he's gotta work at it."

"Did you tell him that?"

"What?"

"Did you tell him what to work on?"

"Look ..." Then I can't hear him for a moment. "... never a coach. I'd appreciate it if you left now; I got a hell of a headache."

"Do you know he came over to see you last night? He pitched in Badger Stadium." Mom pauses, her voice breaking. "He wanted to talk to you, but you were passed out on your goddamn floor, drunk."

"You ever hear of a pitcher named Grover Cleveland?"

I lean in and Mom is staring at him.

"No."

The Pitcher picks up his Skoal and fattens his lip. "Grover pitched for the Cardinals and was a drunk. He was forty. In the second game of the World Series he had to go out and pitch against the Yankees. Tony Lazzeri and everybody couldn't figure out this old washed-up guy could strike out Lazzeri. But he did. He fanned him. "

Mom leans forward.

"What is your point?"

The Pitcher leans back and looks up at her.

"My point is that they asked him how he felt, winning the game, and Grover said if he had blown it, the same guys would have called him a bum who called him a hero. He said he had nothing to prove to anybody." He pauses. "I don't have nothin' to prove either ... to you or anybody else."

I close my eyes. The moon no longer beams down on someone going to make the high school team. It shines on a Mexican kid who doesn't have a chance. I look again and Mom is wiping her eyes.

"You are his coach!"

"Lady ... you don't want a coach ... you're looking for a father."

"*Bullshit*. Who helped you when you needed it? "

"Nobody helped me. I helped me."

"What about your father?'

The Pitcher looks up at her.

"He was a drunken bum who only came back to steal our clothes and our money."

"I would think you'd understand then."

"I don't owe nobody nothing."

Mom steps close, punching the air with her finger.

"I'm going to tell you what you are going to do, because apparently nobody ever has. You are going to sober up and help a boy with his dream. I expect you back at that field tomorrow morning and if you don't come back, I will come over here and personally kick your ass!"

And then Mom walks out the garage and across the street. I follow her and she goes straight into her bedroom and slams the door. I stand in the kitchen and stare at the medical bills on the table. I know she's been trying to find someone who will see her without insurance. And now she has this to worry about.

I walk back to her room.

"Hey ... Mom?"

I'm about to knock when I hear her crying. I stand there not moving, with my head against the door. It breaks your heart, man, to hear your mom cry like that.

20

SO I'M BACK ON THE bench waiting for the Pitcher, with the birds in the trees and the sun creeping over the infield. It's already warm and Mom is smoking. She looks at her watch every few minutes and makes these ticking noises. She looks across the field a couple times, but I know he isn't coming. Like the Pitcher said to me once, *It's your game and nobody else's.* So he must have figured it was his game and that's why I know he isn't coming.

"Let's go," Mom says, standing up. We start across the field and she puts her hand on my shoulder. "We don't need him."

We reach home and I notice his garage door is all the way down. I would have settled for just hearing his ballgame. So then things just sort of go back to normal. Mom and I watch a lot of sport movies. We watch *Rudy*, *The Natural*, and *Field of Dreams*. We watch *Billy Elliot*. Mom loves movies where the characters win after having everything stacked against them. Eventually the Pitcher's garage goes back up and Shortstop sleeps on the drive. Joey and I throw stuff under the garage again. Joey says I should throw an M-80 under his garage for the way he quit on me. I don't know.

The tryouts are getting closer and everyone wants playing time. Devin puts me in when he gets in tight spots. Mrs. Payne talks to him and then *boom,* I come right back out. They want me to just go away, and I think that's why they left the team. It happened when we were playing the Yankees. They had been blasting Eric's fastball out of the park. I didn't think Devin was going to do anything, but then he did something amazing. He pulled Eric and put me in.

Mrs. Payne came charging into the dugout. Mom told me the rest.

"I want to know why Eric is sitting down while *he's* pitching!"

Devin turned to his wife and frowned.

"Beth, they were hitting on Eric! I had to do something."

Mrs. Payne stood in the dugout with her hair pulled back and her eyes bulging.

"Oh, give me a break! Eric happens to get a few hits and you yank him because his pushy Mexican mother harps on you so much!"

Mom said Devin turned bright red then.

"I couldn't keep him in—" he sputtered. "We were going to lose the game!"

Ms. Payne shook her finger.

"Get Eric back out there or we are leaving the team."

That's when the whole *leaving the team thing* started. I didn't know you could leave your *own* team, but in league ball, man, anything can happen. Devin just stared at her.

"What are you talking about?"

Ms. Payne stepped up close, her brow pimpled with sweat, her face sunburned from thousands of baseball games. "Put Eric back in there or we are going to Tri City. My son is the starting pitcher or we leave!"

She said it like a law and Devin gestured wildly to the field. Mom said he paced back and forth in the dugout, trying to explain why I had to keep pitching. But Mrs. Payne just kept shaking her head, telling him that Eric had to pitch or that was it.

"We can't do that now, Beth," he exploded, shaking his head. "The tournament is coming up!"

Mrs. Payne crossed her arms.

"Pull him out now or I am going to get Eric and we are *leaving!*"

Mom said Devin started wavering then and she had to say something.

"You can't pull him, Devin."

That's when Mrs. Payne got in her face.

"Yes he can, he is *the head coach*, and he can do anything he wants! You people think you can have anything you want," she shouted and started throwing gloves, bats, balls, kicking the dirt. "That's it! Eric! Get your bag. We're leaving!"

Eric looked up from the bench and stared at his mother.

"Mom—"

"I know what is best! GET YOUR BAT BAG!"

Eric grabbed his bag and Mrs. Payne sneered at Mom in this low voice.

"You people will be hearing from the league commissioner, because I have a little surprise for you!"

And then Eric and his mother stomped out of the dugout. Mom said Devin stared at them, then shrugged and handed her the clipboard. And that's how the Paynes left the team and that's how Mom became the coach of the Marauders.

Crazy, right?

But that's baseball.

21

I'M READING JOE TORRE'S *THE Yankee Years* when Mom walks in. It's been taking me a while, but all books take a long time with me. I'm reading about how Roger Clemens got ready to pitch. He would put himself in a whirlpool at the highest possible temperature, then when he was lobster red, he had a trainer rub super-hot liniment on his groin. He would start snorting like a bull and then he said he was ready to pitch. I mean, *come on.* Would a guy really do that before a game? But Joe Torre's and Clemens's trainer swear by it.

Mom and I haven't really talked about what happened at the game. I mean her being the coach and all. I was excited because she could play me more, but Mom doesn't roll that way. She doesn't play coach's ball and favor her kid over everyone else. She wants to make sure everyone gets a chance. If anything, she plays me less to not show any favoritism.

"What are you up to there, champ?"

"Just reading."

Mom looks at my picture of No. 27 Juan Marichal, his left leg vertical and his arm coiling like a slingshot. That dude could hurl, man. He'd come over the top with a four-seam fastball that could bust in at one hundred miles an hour. I've watched videos of him on YouTube. He threw so hard he'd skid in the grass after the pitch. If I had been a kid in the sixties, he'd a been my main man.

Mom looks at the trophies we've won over the years and the pictures of my in-house ball teams. She's in every one of them. I still have the tickets from Wrigley Field tacked on my bulletin board from the games. She stares for a moment, then turns. I feel something bad coming the way she clasps her hands, her eyes taking my temperature.

"How's the book?"

I look down with my finger on the Roger Clemens *liniment on balls* part.

"Good."

I thought she might say something about the crazy e-mail from Mrs. Payne. She had sent this e-mail about how the Marauders were the worst team in the league. "*And to use the pushy tactics of the oppressed minority player is just BS ... clearly benching the starting pitcher to placate certain coaches screaming about Mexican rights when the rights of hard working white Americans are being trampled on. My son has been the victim of reverse discrimination and I intend to register complaints with the baseball commissioner. This isn't over ... not by a long shot.*"

Mom says Mrs. Payne has really lost her mind. There is a link called *Americanstokeepillegalsout.com* where you can see if someone is here illegally. I got kind of a chill when I saw the link. Like there are people out there hunting for us.

"I'm sorry that Mr. Langford is not going to coach you anymore, Ricky," she begins, looking at me.

I put the book down and shrug.

"Yeah ... that's alright."

"I think we just have to be thankful he coached you when he did. We'll find someone else," Mom says, trying to put the mom-spin on it. But I don't see how that's going to happen. I hear Mom crying to Grandma about not being able to pay her medical bills. We get these calls all the time from these guys asking for money. And Grandma cries because she thinks they are going to send her back to Mexico. It's like those old movies where the Germans are hauling people off to concentration camps or something.

"That's cool. I'll get on the team anyway," I say, because I figure she has enough to worry about.

Mom's eyes get wet.

"I'm proud of you for that attitude, Ricky." She then stands and pulls back her hair, scratching the corner of her mouth. "I want you to know ... there is a rumor that Eric is playing for Tri City."

I stare at her. "How could Eric manage to get on the Tri City team this late?"

"It's just what I heard."

"That has to be BS, Mom."

Mom's face turns red and then I know, man. I just know. Worse than that, *the freshman coach's kid plays for Tri City!*

"Don't tell me he's pitching for them?"

Mom stands there tight-lipped.

"Eric is pitching for Tri City! Nobody at the end of the season comes in and becomes a starting pitcher, Mom!"

She just stands there with her eyes telling me it's true. Tri City is the best league team in Jacksonville. It's Gino's team. Practically everybody who's on Tri City makes the high school team. We might even face Tri City in the final tournament at the high school field.

"Let's just concentrate on getting you ready for the tryouts," Mom says. "We can't worry about things we can't control."

I stare at her.

"But Mom, what if we end up playing Tri City?"

"Let's cross that bridge when we come to it."

"Oh man, I am screwed," I wail, covering my eyes.

There is no way I can get around this one. With Eric pitching for Tri City and me without a coach, I might as well not go to the tryouts. He is going to sail from pitching for Tri City right to pitching on the freshman team. It is that simple.

"Let's just see what happens, Ricky," Mom says quietly, walking to the door.

"Mom!"

She turns around by the door.

"Do you think ... I mean, man, do you think ... there's any chance the Pitcher might still coach me?"

Mom breathes heavily.

"There's always a chance, Ricky."

I listen to her go down the hall, then stare at *The Yankee Years* and think of Roger Clemens. Go ahead. Put the hottest liniment in the world on my groin. Just let me make the high school team. Straight up. I won't even cry.

22

I TAKE THE BALL AND set my hands. This is where the world falls into order. I breathe and kick back high like Satchel Paige and windmill over the top. I know right away I released too early and the ball sails over Mom's head and rings the backstop. She stands up in her catcher gear and picks the ball up and throws it back. There's really nothing she can say. I'm just getting worse and worse.

Mom and I are back to the Internet printouts. I should hold the ball this way for a sinker or that way for a knuckle ball. None of it works, but like I said, Mom isn't a person who gives up on anything. I keep launching it for the moon. Mom is telling me to square my shoulder and tuck my glove and pick a spot and all the stuff the Pitcher would say. But with Mom it just feels like noise.

"Don't talk when I'm pitching!"

"You need someone to talk to you because you obviously still can't pitch," she shouts back, squatting down behind home plate. We are freaking. The tournament is next week and the tryouts are the week after that. Mom is tired from looking for a job and she's getting sicker.

"Maria, this is Dr. Aziz, please call me as soon as possible."

These messages keep popping up on our phone.

"Well, the tests came back from the hospital," the doctor said on the phone with me on the extension. "Your kidneys are not doing well. Because of the lupus your body is attacking them and that accounts for the blood in your urine and I imagine you have abdominal pain as well. We should probably get you into a dialysis program and do further tests."

That's what the doctor said a few weeks ago. I listened in because I know Mom won't tell me anything. And I want to know why she's sleeping so much and gets tired when we throw the ball. A lot of times at dinner she leaves her plate full and drinks a Diet Coke and goes out to smoke a cigarette. Then today, the doctor calls again.

"When your disease takes a turn like this we have to be very careful. We might have to look at a kidney transplant."

"Whoa, Whoa, Whoa ..."

Mom is in the kitchen. She's drinking her Diet Coke and lighting a cigarette and trying to see if I'm around. She lowers her voice.

"A transplant? No way!"

Mom doesn't take anything from anybody. So hearts, lungs, kidneys are not going to happen if they're coming from somebody else. I could have told the doctor she was wasting her time.

"The pathology of lupus in this stage is that your body will keep attacking your organs until they fail."

"So then, I'm screwed," Mom says quietly.

And I feel my face get hot and my eyes start to burn. But the doctor is silent for a moment. "There are new drug therapies we can try, hormone treatments and like I said, we can make up for the inefficiencies of your kidneys with dialysis. But we have to get aggressive right now and stop your body from attacking your organs or it will cause your organs to fail."

I feel better. Yeah. They can do something for her. Mom just has to play ball with them.

"How long, doc?"

"What?"

"How long do I have?"

"I don't understand."

I don't either. Why does she keep talking like that? She should go in there and get help. But Mom is stubborn, in case you haven't noticed. She has to do things her way.

"I want to know how many months I have before you stick me in a hospital."

I hear her sit down at the kitchen table. I know this doctor is trying to figure her out. The doctor probably has a good family, a husband, a good profession, health insurance. She doesn't know anything about not having health insurance or being worried about losing your house. Hey, if you're not poor, then you don't want to know about being poor.

"Look, doc, my son has high school baseball tryouts," Mom continues. "I have to get him ready to pitch and I can't be spending my time in hospitals going through dialysis and waiting around for a kidney that might never come. I'm going to use the time I have left." She pauses, her voice breaking. "So ... so I just need to know how long I have?"

The doctor breathes real heavy.

"Why would you do that to yourself, Maria?"

Yeah. *Why would you?* I almost say.

Mom speaks in this calm voice. "If you could give your boy his dream, wouldn't you?"

I hang up. I don't want to hear anymore. It sounds like she is going to die. So that's why I call Dr. Aziz back after Mom hangs up. I have to do something. I go outside where the heat is rolling off the street. Mom is watching television. I find the number on the caller ID and hit the redial out in the driveway.

"This is Dr. Aziz," this voice says with a slight accent.

I clear my throat.

"Yeah ... uh, my name is um, Ricky Hernandez," I begin unsteadily.

"Oh ... yes?"

"Yeah ... um ... I've been listening to your messages, you know, " I continue with my heart hammering away. "I see ... yes, yes, I just spoke with her."

"Yeah ... and ... and I wanted to call to find out ... what's wrong with her. " My mouth is really dry now. "She pukes a lot ... I think ... I think she's pretty sick."

There is silence on the phone. I'm staring at this green lizard hanging out on the side of a palm tree. They are pretty cool. They just stay there upside down and wait for insects. Wish I could do that.

"What can I do for you, Ricky?"

"Yeah ..." I swallow. "I want ... I want to like, you know, I want to know ... like, what's wrong with her."

The cell phone is silent against my ear. I have never really talked to a doctor before. I stare across the street at Shortstop asleep on his side. I try to think about something from medical shows like *CSI* where the doctor gives the bad news and everyone starts crying. I just wait outside in the dead heat.

"Ricky ... I can only talk to your mother," Dr. Aziz replies. "I am sorry."

I stare at the Pitcher's garage. I don't know why, but it makes me feel better to know he's in there. Maybe it's just better to know *someone* is around. Fernando was never around; not even drunk in an old garage.

"But please have her call me as soon as possible, so we can help her."

I shut my eyes.

"Can you just tell me this?" I say. "Does what my Mom have

... like, is it ... is it like ... you know ... *life threatening?"*

There is like a really long pause. And I feel like I am not even breathing. *Bump Bump Bump.* That's my heart, man.

"Yes," she says.

Man, I feel weak in my knees, like someone has just kicked my ankles out. I start crying, even though I can't make a sound. My eyes just start watering and my chest is heaving, because I know what she is saying.

"Please have your mother call me and we can make her better, OK?"

"Yeah."

I wipe my eyes and hang up. I look at the garage and hear the Pitcher's ballgame. I think about us not having any medical insurance. The heat hangs on the street like it's on fire and I see one of my baseballs in the yard. They say Cy Young used to pitch so hard he would tear the grandstands apart when the balls flew wild. A reporter said the grandstands looked like a cyclone hit them and that's how he got the name, the *Cyclone.* That's how hard I threw the baseball at his garage. You know, like a cyclone was behind it.

I'll bet the Pitcher jumped straight up.

23

I'M ON THE PORCH READING about Zambrano getting ninety million bucks for pitching for the Cubs. So that got me thinking. Back in the seventies they didn't pay dudes that much, but the Pitcher played a long time. Now they pay guys a million bucks who never even play. Back then players played for teams and free agency hadn't cranked up salaries to where players are now "banks" as the Pitcher called them. I figure Mom isn't going to the doctor because we don't have the money. And if the Pitcher played in the majors for like twenty-five years ... anyway, I figure it's worth a shot

So I pick up the medical bills and walk across the street. Shortstop doesn't even look up as I stand outside the garage with the papers in my hand. I wipe my hands on my shorts, then knock on the peeling wood. I breathe in the old heated tar of his drive. I can barely hear because my heart is slamming in my chest. I knock again. The ballgame rises up and down like a rainstorm. I chip away some paint from his garage door, then slip under.

I can't see a thing. It's like I'm in a dungeon, but then my eyes adjust. I see the Pitcher watching the game. It looks like the Orioles and the Cardinals. I clear my throat.

"Mr. Langford?"

He turns around, then jumps up. He covers his mouth with his hand, blowing smoke into the TV light.

"You throw that goddamn baseball against my garage?"

I shrug.

"Yeah."

He stares at me like I have just barfed. *Bam Bam Bam.* My heart is pitching fastballs. The Pitcher stares at me like I'm some kind of alien. Who would do something like that and then come ask for money?

"What in *the hell* would make you do that?"

"I dunno," I mumble, shrugging again.

"Well, you must want something to do a rockhead thing like that," he says as he walks back and stares at the television.

The Cardinals just got a hit and he's examining the screen like a doctor. I can't think of anything to say. I really just want to go back outside. But then I think of Mom and don't move. The Pitcher watches the game up until a commercial, then turns.

"You still here?"

"Yeah."

"So, what the hell is it you want?"

I stare at Mom's medical bills gnarled in my hand. And like I've never even asked someone for a hundred dollars and now I'm going to ask this dude for *seven grand?* I really had gone loco as Mom says. Who else would go ask some dude in his garage for money after they wailed a baseball against his door? *Nobody.* Except Ricky Hernandez. The Pitcher stares at me, trying to decide which part of my head I fell on. I can hear his fan, the ballgame. I can even hear Shortstop breathing.

Then he turns back to the television.

"You want a Coke or something ... you look hot."

"Yeah."

He walks to his refrigerator and gets a Coke and motions to his footstool. I sit down and the Pitcher settles into his brown La-Z-Boy and cracks open a beer. I drink that Coke like water, man. He holds his beer down and squints at me.

"What the hell's in your hand?"

I look at the medical bills. It seems crazy now to ask him for money.

"Those bills?"

I look down.

"Yeah, they're Mom's medical bills," I mumble

"Let me see them," he says, holding out his hand.

I hand the bills over and the Pitcher lights another cigarette and kicks off his old loafers. Funny thing is he reached for some thick-framed glasses. One time during practice he said, "Do you see that hawk up there?" I stared at the sky and couldn't see anything. And it was then I saw this faint little cross. "How do you know he's a hawk?" He looked at me. "I can see his talons."

The Pitcher holds the papers down in his lap and takes off his glasses.

"Seven thousand bucks they want?"

I nod. Now I know I was nuts to even *think* I could ask for the money. But he saw my play and there is no going back now. The Pitcher whistles, then hands the papers back to me and turns to the game.

"That ain't chump change, buddy."

I feel the nervousness creep up. *How do you ask somebody for seven thousand dollars?* I thought of Mom in her bedroom. The Pitcher said it was *my time* to step up to the plate and that it was *my game* and no one else's. *The batter thinks it his, the ump thinks it his, the manager thinks it's his, but it's your game. You are the pitcher.*

"That why you came over here?"

I nod sheepishly, looking down.

"Mom doesn't know I came over, but ..." I shut my eyes and will my mouth to move. "I was wondering ... I was wondering if you could, you know, lend us the money ... so we could pay Mom's medical bills ... she's sick and won't go to the doctor ... because we don't have the money," I finish.

And my words just hang out there like heavy balloons, man. Like they are waiting to be popped and the Pitcher has the needle. He holds the cigarette by his cheek.

"What's wrong with your mom?"

"She has lupus."

He takes this long, slow drag on his cigarette. The smoke pillows and curls around the television. He flicks the ash.

"I'd like to help you, son. I really would." He shakes his head slowly. "But your mother would never take it from me. She's a proud woman."

I feel encouraged. He hasn't thrown me out of his garage and asked me if I have lost my mind. So that's why I push him a little.

"We could do it and she wouldn't have to know."

"I'm sorry. I just can't," he says.

I nod and put the empty Coke bottle on the table next to his chair. I didn't really believe he would give us the money. I just got my hopes up when he gave me a Coke. *A Coke? Seven Grand? Right?* I stand up and stare at that World Series picture one more time.

"How come ..." I turn to him. "How come you never had a change-up?"

The Pitcher leans back and says cool as November, "I never needed one."

24

WE ARE BACK IN THE streets practicing for the tryouts. Shortstop is snoozing on his back. The Pitcher's television drones in the background as Mom and I throw the ball. When Mom said she wanted to practice in the street, I knew why. If you don't have hope, then what do you have, she always says. But I didn't see it. The Pitcher is done with us. A dude that never wanted to change enough to develop a slower pitch in twenty-five years in the majors isn't going to start changing now.

I work hard and start to get some control back in my arm. We have been practicing about an hour when I really start hitting it. Mom is hunched down in the street and I'm drilling the ball into her mitt with a *pop*. She doesn't turn away from my pitches. I know she has the catcher gear and everything, but a lot of dudes turn away from a seventy-five-mile-an-hour pitch. We are joking and she's calling me Carlos. A warm evening breeze plays down the street and for a moment, the world is behaving.

And then we hear Fernando.

Rat a tat tat. His Harley sounds like him, you know, all explosions. He rolls in all greased back with his shades, feet up on the high pegs with his arms pumped. Like I said, if they make a bad movie about dads who go off and come back like *wannabe gangbangers,* that would be Fernando. He rolls in our drive and kicks down, leaning his bike. It's really quiet when he kills the motor. Mom pulls off her mask as he calls out.

"Hey ... how's the Pitcher, man?"

"Good," I mumble, breathing in booze from his ghetto hug.

Fernando has dark glasses on, but I know his eyes are bright and glittery.

"Yo hey, baby," he says while Mom glares.

She stops in front of him like a cop.

"What are you doing here, Fernando? I don't have any money."

He smiles, flexing his arms over his head. He's all tattoos and earrings along with his Doc Martens and wallet chain. All I can think is this dude watches way too much television, man.

"Oh you know, man, I just came to help my son pitch." He lowers his glasses. "I hear the Pitcher dude said later on him, huh?"

Mom waves him away, her chin moving.

"That's none of your business."

I had to wonder, man, how he would know this. Of course Fernando manages to find out things that there is *no way* you think he would know. He's like the CIA of deadbeat dads or something and he just comes around for all the bad times. I know pitching is over for the day, because I sense he's going to start some shit with Mom.

"Hey, man. Yo, hey, let's see that arm, bro. Throw me a couple," he says, taking my mitt.

Mom steps in front of him. He's already kicking his leg up and pulling the ball in like he's Zambrano or something. Yeah, he's high or drunk, because he almost falls over when he kicks his leg up. I wish we had some money just to make him get back on his Harley and split. But last night we had mac and cheese again and so I know we are really tight.

"Get the hell out of here, Fernando," Mom shouts, coming at him.

"Hey *chill*, baby, chill. I'm just going to throw the ball with my son," he says, moving like a fighter. He turns to me. "You go down, man, and I'll throw you some pitches. I'll coach you, man."

I don't move and Fernando nods, pulling back his arm, loosening up.

"Go on, man," he urges. "I'm as good as that dude. I'm the dude that should be teaching you anyway, not that old washed-up motherfu----. I'll just throw you a couple and show you the way man."

He's kicking up his leg again like's he's in the majors, muttering, "Yeah, this feels good, feels right!"

Mom shakes her head and throws me the catcher's glove.

"Let the asshole pitch and then maybe he'll leave," she says.

I walk off into the distance and squat down in the hot street. I don't want to do this. Fernando is like a bad flu that keeps coming back. I can smell the oily tar as I hold my mitt. I'm hoping like he'll throw a couple and take off. He usually loses interest pretty fast whenever we play ball.

"Alright, man. Get ready," Fernando calls out. "Here comes my fastball, bro." He kicks up and I have to grab it out of the air. But here's the thing, man—the ball came in like a blooper. No heat at all. I mean, here's big bad Fernando with his tats and muscles and his Harley, and he throws a ball like forty miles an hour.

He's moving his arm in a circle and frowning.

"Hey, man ... let me do it again," he calls. "I'm just rusty, bro."

Mom shakes her head and laughs.

"That's your fastball?"

"Quiet, bitch," he mutters.

I squat down again and hold up my mitt. Fernando does his crazy-ass windup with his foot kicking up to the moon. He nearly falls over and the ball floats in even slower and thuds in my mitt. I throw it back and grin.

"I thought you were throwing a fastball, man?"

Fernando glares at me, rubbing his shoulder.

"You think it's funny?"

Fernando is a dude who doesn't like to be laughed at. Mom is covering her mouth and I'm looking away. Maybe it's the whole age thing. He always talked about how he was this bad-ass pitcher and maybe he was. But not now, bro. He throws in another slow ball and Mom laughs again and his face turns red. He wings the ball back to me.

"Alright, you little shit. Let's see your fastball!"

All Fernando, right? He hunches down and slaps his mitt.

"Come on, man. You think you so bad now with your pitching. I notice, man, that the Pitcher dude didn't think you were *so bad*, bro. You think you better than me." He hits his mitt again. "You can't even hit the zone, man. You ain't shit."

That stings. I mean, what kind of dad would say that? Like I said, I quit thinking about him as my dad a long time ago. I don't know, man, maybe all the times he beat Mom and hit me and took our money came together. Maybe I was just tired of all the trouble he causes every time he comes around. Like the night on the patio where he tried to kill me. So maybe that's why I pick his right knee.

Like the Pitcher said, there ain't nothing but the spot.

"You got no heat!" he shouts. "Come on and we'll see who laughs at who, you little fag! You think you better than me. You just nothing, man! You got no arm! If you had an arm, man, that dude would still be coaching you!"

I listen to this shit and set myself. Fernando is hitting his glove. I breathe in, close my eyes, and feel the world go quiet. I'm on. I can feel it. I kick back into my windup with my shoulder square, pushing off my back leg, tucking my glove, whipping over my head like a windmill. I hear the crack man. I hit my spot perfectly.

And Fernando goes down.

"Motherf-----! MOTHERF-----!"

He's cussing and holding his knee in the street. Mom gives me a high-five while Fernando rolls on the ground. Then Mom gives me a knuckle bump.

"Nice pitch, Ricky!"

I probably hit a personal best with that pitch, you know. Then suddenly Fernando is up. I don't know if he is drunk or adrenaline is pumping through him or what. But he jumps up and starts charging down the street like a raging bull.

"You little bastard! You did that on purpose!"

I start booking down the street. Fernando is fast and catches my shirt. He pulls me and draws back as I duck. His fist smacks the side of my jaw anyway. *Pow!* Like someone smacking you with a bat. You ever get up too fast and the world gets fuzzy and kind of dark? That's what it's like when Fernando hits you. I hit the pavement with blood warm and salty in my mouth

"You f------ asshole, don't you hit my son. You f------ asshole!"

Mom is swinging and clawing and Fernando is blocking her.

"Don't you hit me, bitch!"

I see Mom trying to strangle Fernando and then he hits her. *Pow!* She falls to the street like a rag doll. He tries to pick her up and that's when I see the Louisville Slugger swing through the twilight. I hear that *whooonh* sound a bat makes when you take practice swings. The bat catches Fernando under his ribcage and he goes down to the pavement. He hold his hands up and starts crabbing backward.

"DON'T YOU F------ HIT ME, MAN!"

The Pitcher draws back and smashes Fernando's shoulder,

like one of those pottery bowls. He screams out like a girl and is hugging the street. Then Fernando is crawling as the Pitcher lines up and hits his other knee with a chop. He screams again and cries out.

I think the Pitcher would have killed him if Mom hadn't stopped him. Besides, the cops, the fire trucks, and paramedics had arrived by then.

And all hell broke loose.

25

Picture this: After the swirling lights and sirens and cops and stretchers, Mom and I are standing outside the Pitcher's garage with a steaming plate of fajitas. She's in her blue flowery dress with the spaghetti straps (that's her word, not mine) and high heels and a flower in her hair and her perfume hangs in the warm air. I'm holding a glass of ice tea with my bandaged jaw and Mom is there with her bandaged eye.

I bet we look pretty funny to somebody else.

After the police left Mom started cooking. I hope I don't forget anything, but here's how it went down after the Pitcher busted up Fernando. About five cop cars pulled up and it looked like a battlefield with me bleeding and Mom holding her eye and Fernando crawling in the street. He couldn't move too good because of his busted knees and shoulder and busted ribs. He screamed *F---!* over and over and the cops didn't know what to do.

They were probably like, *Mexicans*, right?

The Pitcher told them what went down and the ambulance took Fernando away. The cops charged him with domestic battery and basically trying to kill us. The paramedic dudes wanted us to go the hospital, but we were alright. Mom had been beat worse by Fernando and I guess I have too—although he hit me pretty hard this time. They bandaged us up and everybody left.

It is kind of weird, man. One moment the neighborhood is full of ambulances and police cars with lights swirling all over the place. Even a fire truck came and the fireman stood around and talked to the cops who talked to the paramedics who talked to us. And the neighbors were out, I mean people you never see, man, like the Gumpers, and old man Henderson, and the Donnellys, and the old lady Messolini, and Jimmy's family. But then everyone just went back in their houses.

That's when Mom stared at the Pitcher's garage. I think it was because she hadn't been able to thank him. She put on her dress, her heels, her perfume, the flower in her hair, and whipped up the fajitas, then handed me the ice tea. Then we headed across the street.

So now we are standing outside the garage. Mom knocks on the chipped door and says in a loud voice:

"Mr. Langford, I have brought you over some dinner!"

Just like before, the television goes low and I can hear him walking. I am wondering if he will come out. Maybe he figures he's done with the crazy-ass Mexicans, you know. But the garage rolls up and Shortstop comes out wagging his tail. The Pitcher is standing there with his cigarette, wearing a red golf shirt. He drops the cigarette and smooths back his hair, staring at Mom with her bandage and swollen eye. She covers her face like the sun is bothering her.

"I want to thank you for what you did for us," she says, keeping her hand over her eye. "I guess I'm always thanking you for something," she murmurs.

"No problem," he says, moving his loafer on the cement.

But I can tell he's embarrassed.

We stand there and nobody can think of anything to say. It is like every common thing you can talk about has gone away. Maybe there is nothing to say anymore. So Mom holds up the plate.

"I made you dinner," she says, handing him the fajitas with a napkin. "I put extra peppers on them ... the way you like it."

The Pitcher takes the plate and I notice two red spots on his cheeks. He looks at Mom, his eyes going to the bandage.

"Are you alright?"

"Nothing a little makeup can't hide," Mom says and smiles. "Fernando doesn't hit as hard as he used to."

And I see the Pitcher kind of flinch. But I'm like ... *you think this is a first time, dude?* The cops said Mom could charge him and put him in jail this time. So maybe the hell that is Fernando will be over ... for a while at least.

"Well, thank you again," Mom says, turning around.

"Why don't you stay for a while?"

Mom turns and looks at him and he opens his hand.

"I have a few beers in the refrigerator."

"I'm sure you have other commitments," Mom says, but she isn't messing with him. She's just being polite. And then he says something that just blows me away:

"Please."

I didn't know pitchers even *used* that word. Mom hesitates. I think she is trying to not get sucked in again. You know, get our hopes up or anything like that. I mean, it's happened a few times now, you know. The Pitcher pulls up two chairs by the La-Z- Boy and puts the fajitas on the table with his Good Times, Skoal, and cigarettes. The ballgame is on and the night air is flowing in. Mom crosses her legs and I see the Pitcher eyes them. My mom has good legs.

He looks at me.

"You forgot something," he says, reaching over and picking up some papers.

I stare at the documents and feel my face get hot. *How could I have forgotten those papers?* Mom's eyes grow as she recognizes her medical bills, then she turns deep red.

"Ricky!"

"Your son brought these over the other night," the Pitcher explains. "He wanted to help you out."

Mom is looking at the papers, then me, then the papers. She stands up and cries out.

"What are you doing bringing our personal business to this man!"

I have no answer. How do you tell your Mom you went begging for seven grand from your neighbor? Answer: You don't! Because that is not how Mom rolls. She won't ask for anything unless it is for me. But in this case, man, I have Mom's back covered.

"I don't know. I just thought ..."

"Oh Ricky." Mom rubs her forehead, her eyes jamming back and forth. "You ... you didn't ask Mr. Langford for money ... *did you?"*

Now all I want to do is get away. I want to run right out the door, you know. Just run down the street and keep going. The Pitcher takes a bite of his fajita and looks at her.

"He asked for a loan, which is what neighbors do when times get hard."

This does nothing, because Mom is about to spontaneously combust. She's holding her head like she has a terrific headache. She looks up at me with her eyes red.

"That is our personal business, Ricky! You don't ask other people for money!" She turns to the Pitcher. "I am so *sorry,* Mr. Langford. We have taken enough of your time. My son had no right to ask you to loan us money. I would have *never* let him bring our problems to you and—"

"Don't worry about it," he says, cutting her off. "Besides, I paid your bills."

Boom! Just like that. *He paid Mom's medical bills.* I can barely believe my ears. Mom stares at the Pitcher with her mouth half-open. I'm not moving, because I want to make sure I heard him right. Mom's mouth opens and shuts, finally she cries out, *"What!"*

It's like the world just stopped. Mom looks like one of those people who have seen an alien on television.

"I'm sorry." Mom is staring at him, pulling a loose strand of hair back. "What did you say?"

"I said it's too late," he answers, clapping his lighter shut. "I paid your medical bills."

Mom is now like the Wicked Witch of the West when she gets the water thrown on her. *Like she's going to melt right there.* I'm staring at the Pitcher too, because I'm having a hard time believing what he just said. He smokes with the cigarette by his cheek.

"What do you mean?"

The Pitcher rolls his shoulders.

"I figured you needed the help. So I paid the seven grand for you."

Mom's mouth opens, changes shape, makes this sound like, *Ah ... Ah ...*

"ALRIGHT!"

That's me. Yeah. I guess I shouldn't have shouted, but when your Mom is sick, it's like there's a tornado out there, and you know it is getting closer and closer. When the Pitcher said he paid the seven grand it was like a second life. But Mom is staring like she wants to vaporize me. Because in her mind, everything just took a really bad turn for the worse.

"Ricky!"

But I don't care. You don't care who pays what, man, because it just means the worst isn't going to happen. And then, of course, Mom starts crying. Now the Pitcher looks embarrassed. She breathes heavily in her dress with her flower and the bandage on her eye and you can see *the stress* lift. It's like a demon or a gargoyle comes off her shoulders and flaps away into the night. Mom sits back down and puts her hand over her face.

"And another thing, what's this I hear about you not going to the goddamn doctor?"

Mom looks at me with her mascara all inky.

"Ricky!"

I shrug. Hey man. What can I say? She's my mom, man. You do what you have to do, right? *It's your game.* The Pitcher hands her a card and motions with his cigarette.

"Have every bill from the doctor sent to this address," he orders her. "And I want you to go see a doctor."

"No. No." Mom shakes her head. "I can't accept this ... I will pay you back the money."

"No you won't," the Pitcher says flatly. "That's a gift and you *will* accept this card, Maria," he continues, leveling his cigarette. "Or I won't coach your son and I know those high school tryouts are coming up."

Just like that. Mom stares at him, her face red, ink-streaked, and bandaged. I feel like someone has just pumped me full of air. I mean, *did I hear him right? He was going to coach me again?* It is like there is light in the world again. Eric won't destroy me in the championship game and I might still make the high school team. I feel like skipping around the room, man.

"Tryouts are coming up, right?" he asks, turning to me.

"Yeah. Two weeks."

The Pitcher keeps his eyes on Mom with the cigarette by his cheek.

"So that's the deal," he says. "I'll coach your son and I'll make sure he gets on that high school team." He pumps his cigarette toward Mom. "But you get to the doctor, and then let me take you out to a nice restaurant. And don't tell me you are paying me back the goddamn money. That's a gift."

Mom sits there and doesn't move.

"That's blackmail," she says quietly, looking up.

The Pitcher nods.

"Yeah. That's right."

I know he has her then, man. She tries to protest, but the Pitcher says that's the deal. Then he says he will drive her to *the goddamn doctor* himself. And so then Mom gets real quiet again and looks at him like she can't believe any of this. And to tell you the truth, I can't either. The Pitcher went from quitting on me, getting drunk, not showing up, quitting again, to paying Mom's doctor bills and coaching me again. I mean, we are equipped to handle all the bad shit, you know.

But good things are a little trickier.

26

SO WE ARE BACK AT Roland Field and it's hot. The Pitcher doesn't have his cooler of beers and is sweating like crazy. That is Mom's condition on him. If he wants to go to dinner with her then he has to back off on the drinking. Mom says he has been drinking ever since his wife died. That's a lot of Good Times beers. My mind is wandering and the Pitcher is crabby because he wants a beer. He's smoking and spitting chew.

We are like the miserable brothers, you know.

"Alright ... just throw me a fastball," he orders from behind the plate.

I'm watching myself pitch and you don't want to ever watch yourself do anything. So I throw in a bunch of fastballs right over his head. The Pitcher stands up and stares at me.

"What the hell is wrong with you?"

"How should I know."

Only I do know. And it bugs the hell out of me. Maybe because I feel like whatever I do there is someone out there blocking me.

I'm watching the Pitcher explain the pitches all over again and I'm just watching his mouth move. It's like someone turned off the sound.

"You ain't listening, rockhead!"

I watch him stride toward me and start thinking maybe we waited too long. The tournament game against Eric's team is this week. You ever see that old show *I Dream of Jeannie*? I've caught it on TVland a couple of times. Pitching is like when the smoke comes out of Jeannie's bottle and she appears in her bikini outfit. I'm seeing no smoke and definitely *no Jeannie*. Maybe it has all just blown away.

The Pitcher gets right up into my face.

"You ain't focusing on a goddamn word I'm saying," he snaps, pulling a ball out of the bucket. "For a curve you gotta hold it by the seams and bring your arm down and snap your wrist for the rotation. You gotta let your arm do the work, because if that ball don't spin, it ain't going to curve. It's the same with the sinker, if you don't keep it from spinning, it ain't going to do what you want it to."

I look off across the field.

"*Hey!* You listening to me?"

"Yeah!"

But all I can think about is getting something to drink.

"Try a curve and let me see the ball break this time!"

The Pitcher walks back and hunches down. Now I'm seeing Eric laughing at me. *You might as well give it up now, beano. You suck!* He's laughing the way he did when he took my cupcake. I hold the ball, feeling the sun on my neck.

"From the windup," the Pitcher calls.

I set myself, shut my eyes, take my breath, but Eric never leaves. I launch the ball with the fence rattling like a bell at midnight. The Pitcher stands up and looks at the backstop.

"What the hell was that?"

"My curve!"

"My grandmother could throw a better curve than that one!"

"Then let her!"

I am hot and tired and maybe that's why I said what I said. The Pitcher walks up to the mound slowly. His shirt is drenched from the heat. He lights a cigarette with his Zippo and looks off across the ball field. The wind moves the trees and swishes the grass and whips the infield sand. He turns with the cigarette below his mouth.

"What ... you had enough?"

I shrug and pull on some loose rawhide on my mitt. Maybe I had had enough. Maybe I should have never bothered him in the first place. Yeah I can throw fast, but I still don't know how to control my pitch. And I can't stop thinking about other things. Maybe I could never stop thinking about other things. Maybe an arm just isn't enough.

"Maybe."

"You think the guy who is going to take your spot has had enough?"

"How should I know?"

"What was that?"

And there is Eric again. Somehow he has gotten into my head and now even a major league pitcher can't help me. Everything just seems so hard. Like the simplest thing is hard. You ever have that? I get it all the time. So, I snap. It happens when I get pushed.

"I said I don't know!"

The Pitcher frowns.

"What's wrong with you?"

I stare at my mitt and wait for him to tell me to go home. I want to go home and just sleep in the darkness. I am crazy to think I can make the high school team. The real world doesn't care about a seventy-five-mile-an-hour fastball. The real world is giving personal lessons to Eric right now.

I shake my head and kick the dirt.

"Eric is getting coached by the freshman coach," I mutter. "He's getting personal lessons and that's that." I shake my head. "This is all for nothing ... all bullshit."

The Pitcher nods slowly.

"So you're a quitter."

I stare at him.

"Didn't you hear me? Eric is going to be *the pitcher!*"

"Yeah, so what? He call you a wetback or something?"

"No!"

"That's the way you are acting," he continues. "He call you a beano or tell you to get your wetback ass back to Mexico?"

"Nobody called me a wetback!"

He steps up close, getting in my face.

"I'm calling you one now. You're just a wetback who doesn't want to do the goddamn work!"

"Don't call me that!"

"Why not? You're acting like one. You're just another Mexican who doesn't want to do the work to become a pitcher."

Man, I feel like my head is going to blow apart.

"Maybe I can't pitch! *Maybe I don't want to!*"

The Pitcher takes the cigarette from his mouth and looks at me.

"I don't want to waste my time on quitters," he says.

I stare at him, feeling like I have just been punched.

"So, *I'm* a quitter?"

"That's what I see out here," he answers, shrugging. "A Mexican kid who can't handle it when the going gets tough and so he quits. Throws a tantrum and quits."

My heart goes into overdrive.

"Yeah, my mom said the reason you sleep in your garage is because your *wife died* and you don't want anything that reminds you of her!"

"Best you can do there, wetback?" he says.

"Yeah ... so ... *you* quit!" I jab my finger at him. "You started drinking that stupid Good Times beer and you're just a drunk who lives in his garage after winning the World Series! You just feel sorry for yourself because you ... you can't pitch anymore! So don't tell me *I'm* the quitter when *you're* the quitter!"

Then it is just quiet. That's how I know I have been screaming. I figure he will tell the asshole Mexican kid to go home now. But all he does is drop his cigarette and stub it with his cleat. He looks up at me, his eyes calm.

"You gotta be able to take it," he says quietly. "You can't get frustrated or mad. I don't care what anybody calls you or says to you. You got a job to do. You're the pitcher and I don't care if God himself is coaching this kid. You go out there and pitch your guts out every time and give a hundred and ten percent and don't worry about the rest."

I nod, feeling really stupid for what I said.

"So now we got that out of the way. What the hell else is bugging you?"

I shrug. "I need ...," I begin, then trail off.

"Yeah, spit it out, rockhead."

I shake my head.

"I need something Eric doesn't know. He knows how I pitch and he knows how to hit on me." I pause. "I want to learn a change-up."

The Pitcher squints into the distance.

"And you think that's going to help you?"

"It's different."

The Pitcher leans forward, his grey eyes pinning me.

"Different ain't necessarily better."

"Yeah ... but most times it is."

He spits off the mound.

"I pitched twenty-five years in the majors and never needed a change-up. What the hell does that tell you?"

"Maybe you didn't need one."

"That's right, rockhead," he says, nodding. "And you don't

either! You pitch the way I've seen you pitch, hit the corners. You got no worries. I'll get you a curve and a sinker and with your fastball, you'll have no problems ... I never did."

I shut one eye against the sun.

"But what if I'm not like you?"

The Pitcher glances at me, then tips his shoulders.

"Then you ain't lucky."

27

MOM IS ALL SUNSHINE, MAN. She comes out in this black off-the-shoulder number and these jangly earrings. Her perfume smells like the ladies at the church back when we went to church. Except Mom's perfume smells kind of like lemons or something. She is smiling and her teeth are flashing and her eyes look like emeralds. I'm watching a ballgame on the couch when she twirls around in these stiletto heels and her dress fans out like the movies. She stops and looks at me with her hands on her waist.

"So what do you think?"

"Wow!" I sit up on the couch. "You look great, Mom!"

She drills me with her eyes.

"Are you just saying that?"

"Straight up, Mom," I say, nodding. "Beautiful."

And she does. I see guys watching her when we go to the grocery store. Once this dude came up and started talking to us in the Ethnic Food aisle. He had this blond hair and those goofy white guy shorts that are plaid and the little guy with the Polo mallet. He just kept talking and talking and then finally he said, "Maybe we can have coffee sometime?"

Mom looked at him, her eyes sparking. "I'm a married woman, *cabrón*."

And the dude turned red and we got our gallon of milk and got out of there. I asked her why she told him she was married when Fernando had been gone a couple years. Mom said she didn't need the headache. I didn't really know what she meant, but I kind of do. I mean girls are alright, man, but I don't need the headache. I mean between school and baseball, I got my hands full. Still, you know, I can see one day rolling that way.

A lot of dudes already have.

So I look at Mom and she's standing there like a princess waiting to be picked up.

"Are you going out with the Pitcher, Mom?"

"We are just going to dinner," she answers, waving her hand like it's no big deal.

I don't ever remember Mom getting all dressed up and going to dinner with Fernando. I mean he'd take us to Portillo's or McDonald's or Chili's or some greasy beef place where he could make a pig of himself. Or he'd take us to this place and order up hot wings and drink a bunch of beer with all these kids running everywhere. But Mom never got dressed up like this for any of those places.

I watch her in the mirror.

"You like the Pitcher, Mom?"

She turns and jams her hands on her hips.

"We are going to dinner ... *dinner*. He didn't ask me to marry him."

"You never know," I pointed out.

"Don't you have some homework?"

"It's summer, Mom."

"Well read a book from that reading list then."

Just then the doorbell rings and Mom's eyes get big.

"Maybe I should try a different dress," she murmurs. "This might make me look too ethic, you know."

"Too late, Mom," I say going to the door. "Besides, you are ethnic."

She looks at me.

"Where are you going, Ricky?"

"To let him in," I call back.

I go to the door and there's the Pitcher in a blue sport coat and tan slacks and loafers. Kind of like that first night he came to dinner. His hair is combed to the side and I don't know if he shaved, but he looks different.

He downs a can of Good Times and sets it on the porch.

"Hair of the dog," he mutters. "Don't tell your mother."

"I'm coming," Mom shouts and I flatten against the wall as she steps out.

The Pitcher stares at her and his eyes light up.

"You look beautiful, Maria," he says.

That is the first time I have heard him use her name. Alright, maybe the second time, but he usually calls her Ms.Hernandez and she calls him Mr. Langford and I don't know, it sounds good hearing Maria. Mom has this little black purse I have never seen before. And I'm glad, because she looks rich, man. She looks like one of those ladies you see on television.

"We won't be late," Mom calls back as the Pitcher holds the door to his station wagon.

I never saw Fernando do that, man. He would always walk in front of us and never held the door. The Pitcher shuts her door and Mom looks out the window. I wave to her and she waves back like crazy. And they drive off down the street.

So Mom is on a date with a World Series pitcher. Cool. More than that, she's happy. Very cool. You want your mom to be happy, man.

***

I kill time with Ramen Noodles, bowls of ice cream, ESPN, chips, and hours and hours of ballgames. Looks like the Sox are making a run for it with Bobby Jenks closing down the games with that one-hundred-and-two-mile-an-hour fastball. It's so cool to watch Ozzie—he's the coach—make the motion with his hands for *the Big Man*. Bobby Jenks rolls out there and you see him draw back and *wham!* One hundred and two! I mean, come on! This dude is throwing a baseball *one hundred and two miles an hour!* It's cool just to see those numbers on the screen.

I fall asleep on the couch and later, don't even hear them come in. I wake up and it's dark and the television is off. Someone had put a blanket over me. I can hear voices out on the patio and then I hear Mom's laugh. I have never heard her laugh that way before. In that laugh is no illness, man, no stress. There are no worries in that laugh. It sings like the wind and makes you think of wide-open fields or oceans or ski slopes with everybody happy.

"I don't know how to thank you for ..."

The Pitcher is quiet. I know what she's talking about. She can go to the doctor again and that's like a new life. If you ever had it where you can't go get help, then you know what I'm talking about. The Pitcher says something and I hear Mom again

"I want him to make it for him ... he needs this success. He needs it for himself ... I'm afraid if he doesn't get it then he won't have another chance ... for his esteem ... this is his moment to shine ..."

I sit up and see candles flickering under the umbrella. It's bright outside from the moon and Mom is leaning against him. I'm glad. Mom needs someone to lean against. I can hear the wind and some crickets, then I realize she isn't leaning against his shoulder. So I creep into my bedroom. I'm not going to say I hear anything else, but I do. Then I hear the front door open at about *SIX AM!*

I mean ... *Wow!*

Right?

***

OK. I'm going to say it. Mom is dating a *World Series pitcher!* She makes him dinner and they sit out on our patio and drink wine. I wake up sometimes and hear music and they are dancing. I mean not like hip-hop, but like old-movie dancing. Like that tango they did the first night. You know, cheek to cheek. And you know that *six AM thing* of hearing the front door? It starts happening a lot. A couple times I go to the kitchen to throw down some cereal and his old loafers are in the living room with wine glasses on the counter.

And then I hear Mom kind of yelling, but not in a bad way. You know.

They take these walks around the neighborhood and hold hands. It's like they are a married couple. Then they get in his old station wagon and take a drive. Just take a drive. Like what does that even mean, you know? Mom says they get a couple of coffees from Starbucks and drive down to the beach and watch the ocean. *That's fun?* But Mom says she loves it. That's cool, because Mom never had this before with Fernando. She's in this great mood that just seems to go on and on. She's singing to herself and I'm working with the Pitcher and the tournament is coming up. He doesn't get half as grouchy when I launch the ball against the backstop fence.

So I just ask her one day. She is picking up their wine glasses on the patio.

"Hey, Mom," I call out from the couch. "Is like, the Pitcher your boyfriend?"

She pauses with this little smile on her face.

"I'll never tell," she says.

28

WE ARE BACK AT THE baseball field behind the school. The tournament starts tomorrow and then the tryouts are the week after. It's evening and the grass is damp and there is a nice breeze. We have been working on my fastball, my cutter, and a curve, getting the ball to break inside and outside. The Pitcher has a cigarette in the corner of his mouth. His large brown hands move the ball around.

"OK. This pitch is made for you because you got a natural fastball," he says, holding the ball up. "You hold this one between the two seams. Then you throw it and the rotation of the ball builds and it sinks down over the plate, kind of like the curve. You got it? You get the guy to swing up since it's sinking, that's why they call it a sinker, but he only gets a piece of it and hits a grounder. You get him at first; boom, there's your first out. You following me, rockhead?"

"Yeah."

"You aren't out in the clouds or somewhere?"

"Nope."

He spits, looking to first base. We are on the mound and I can see the moon and a first star. A train is clickety-clacking somewhere and the air has cooled.

"Alright. So the next guy comes up and you throw him the same pitch. He gets a piece of it and now you get him at first. Or you get the guy at second. Let's say they both got on and you have a man at first and second now. So you throw another one and he chips at it and now you run for third base, because you gotta get the 'out' there or you get a double play."

The Pitcher takes the cigarette from his mouth.

"Or, you got a guy who figures it out and the best he can do is hit it down the baseline, because it's not coming off his bat square. You still are going to keep him to a single." He stares at me to see if I'm zoning off. "See, you gotta be thinking, 'what next, what next?' You want to be thinking ahead of the guy batting. The rockheads who don't think, they never make it, Ricky. Everybody can throw hard, but you gotta be ready for what comes next. You gotta outthink the batter."

The Pitcher puts the ball in my glove and looks at me.

"I knew a kid once who had a million dollar arm. He could have written his ticket, but he never wanted to work at it. He just wanted to throw fast. He had the arm, but he didn't have it up here." He taps his temple. "Rockheads don't become great pitchers. You gotta use the noodle."

I nod as he picks up his glove.

"I'll catch for you. Don't bean me," he calls back, walking to the plate in his long stride with his old grey sweats and the cleats. Dust trails his shoes and I have this moment where I think I might never see this again. I might never watch an old World Series pitcher turn and squat down behind the plate.

"Alright." He beat his mitt. "Bring it."

I bring my hands together and push back on the rubber.

"Position the ball in your glove. Don't let me see it."

I nod and move the ball.

"Throw it from the windup," he says, right before I kick back.

I nod again, breathe in the night air, then kick back and come over the top. The ball digs into the dirt in front of the plate. The Pitcher catches it on the hop and looks at me.

"What happened there?"

"I don't know," I answer, shrugging.

"You forgot everything I told you! Pitch like you are hitting a man! Follow through! Hold the ball between the seams and get a rotation going. Twist your hand before the release. You can't rely on your natural ability anymore; you gotta try harder now. *Concentrate!*" The Pitcher motions to the sky. "You have been going along thinking that God or whoever will just let you pitch a hundred-mile-an-hour fastball. *You* gotta to do it now. You gotta pitch up a level."

"You say gotta a lot," I shout.

He throws me the ball.

"Shut up and try it again."

I take the ball and bring my hands together. I take a breath, then kick back and come over the top for a fastball, but the ball rings the backstop. The Pitcher holds up his hand and walks to the mound.

"Alright, what the hell is going on?"

"I dunno ..."

"Did you pick a spot?"

"I guess I forgot."

He spits a stream of tobacco juice.

"You'd forget your head if it wasn't attached, wouldn't you?"

"Yeah ..." I shrug. "Probably."

The Pitcher stares at me.

"You forget a lot of things, don't you?"

He asks the question like a doctor. I feel like I'm back in school with the teacher telling me for the hundredth time to pay attention. I look down at the ground, punching my mitt.

"I'm dyslexic," I say.

"What the hell is that?"

"I have trouble with words, I guess," I mumble, feeling my face get hot. "I forget a lot of stuff."

The Pitcher breathes heavily, pushing his hat back.

"Well anybody that can get somebody to give them seven grand ain't dumb, kid."

I smile a little and shrug.

"Yeah ... maybe."

"Listen, Koufax couldn't remember nothing and Dizzy Dean couldn't even spell *school*. You don't gotta be a brain surgeon to pitch. Look at me," he says, touching his chest. "I ain't no Einstein and I barely finished high school, but I pitched twenty-five goddamn years in the majors. Let's see Einstein do that!" He nods. "You are plenty smart enough, don't worry about that."

I feel better. Mom says it doesn't do any good to dwell, you know. She says you just gotta go on and do the best you can. So I am glad to hear the Pitcher didn't do so well in high school either. I knew Bobby Jenks flunked out of high school and became ineligible. I'm not saying that's the way I roll; I'm just saying it feels better to know there are other dudes like me out there.

"Everybody has something kid," the Pitcher continues, putting the ball in my mitt. "I got a disability that makes yours look like a little boy whining about a blister. I had to learn to pitch with rocks. Try that some time."

"Is that why we threw rocks, because that's how you learned?"

"No. I had to get you to forget yourself, which is *not* what you are doing now. So here is what we are going to do." He taps his shirt. "I want you to concentrate on this pack of cigarettes in my pocket. You got it? I don't care what else you do. Just concentrate on these cigarettes and make sure the ball goes there. That's all you are going to think about. Got it?"

"Yeah. Just your pack of cigarettes," I repeat.

"That's right."

The Pitcher walks back to the plate and kneels down slowly.

"You gotta get it right, kid, because my knees are about to give out."

I bring my hands together and set myself. I take my breath and everything disappears. I can hear the wind in the trees. I keep my eyes on his pocket and see the outline of the cigarettes and how they weigh down his shirt. I breathe again, kick back, bring up my arm, tuck my glove, then follow through, twisting my wrist for a sinker.

The ball screams in toward the Pitcher, then breaks down into his glove.

He nods slowly, still framing the ball.

"Better."

29

We sit outside the Pitcher's garage. Game day: butterflies, sunflower seeds, peanuts, water bottles, Gatorade, bat bags, PowerBars, batting gloves, shades, cleats and lots of dust. I'm always tense on game day and I can tell Mom is tense too. She smokes with her lips crinkling and the lines around her eyes inflating like ridges in a dry desert. Ash falls into her lap as she looks at her watch.

"Go see if he's up," she says, nodding.

I get out of the car and walk across the short grass and hear his television. We had waited for the Pitcher to come over all morning and then Mom just said to get in our van. Neither of us wanted to say the obvious. That the Pitcher might have gone back to his old ways. It was like having a light that just wouldn't stay on.

So now I'm standing outside his door and I can hear two guys from ESPN debating the merits of the infield fly rule. I lean down.

"Mr. Langford?"

I don't hear anything and look at Mom. She motions me to go under the garage. I slip under and it's dark, then my eyes adjust. The Pitcher has this pull out bed folded from a couch. I walk over and see a bunch of Good Times cans on the cement. Cigarettes litter the floor. The Pitcher is half-off the bed, snoring face down.

"Mr. Langford?"

I stand next to him, breathing the booze from his breath. It's then I see he's in his underwear with one sock on. I look up at the pictures on the wall. He's still winning the World Series, jumping into his catcher's arms, and here he is drunk in his underwear. I stare at him and for the first time the pictures don't seem to matter anymore.

"Where is he?" Mom demands when I get back in the car.

"Asleep," I mutter, shutting the door.

Her eyes pin me.

"Asleep? What do you mean he's *asleep?*"

"He's asleep," I mumble. "In his bed."

Mom stares at me.

"He was drunk, wasn't he?"

"Can we just go, Mom. *Please* ... let's just go," I say, looking straight ahead.

Mom looks at the garage, then swears under her breath and puts the van in gear. I know how she feels, man, because I feel the same way. Mom glances at me and I look away. She wipes her eyes, driving faster.

"That bastard," she mutters, speaking for both of us.

30

WE PULL UP AND SEE the Payne's shiny black van with a yellow DON'T TREAD ON ME bumper sticker. Mrs. Payne lets Eric out like he's a rock star and gives us the Mexican Death Stare. They head toward the field with a monster thermos of Gatorade and two folding chairs with canopies. They are like the baseball family and Eric looks like a pitcher. You never want to admit to those feelings, man, but they are there.

Mom stubs her cigarette and we get out of the car. She's worried. It's the first game she's coaching by herself and it doesn't help that the Pitcher got drunk again and blew us off. I don't even want to think about it because I have to concentrate on the game. Really, it feels like the day Fernando left, which is weird because the Pitcher is not my dad. Mom carries her clipboard with the scorebook under her arm and doesn't say a word. I'm lugging the equipment bag like a drunk.

We walk silently toward the baseball field.

***

Now we are in the high school field. A Mexican dude is watering the grass while other guys rake the infield. There's not a cloud in the sky and the scoreboard is huge and says SOUTH WILDCATS BASEBALL. This is the last stop on the train to high school baseball. This is where we have all been heading since Coach Devin declared the mission of his team—*"to get you boys ready for high school ball."* That was BS of course; it was to get Eric ready for high school ball. But still, everyone is jacked.

The stadium doesn't seem like league ball with concrete dugouts and a heavy fence that keeps fans from the players. People are handing bottles of Gatorade through the mesh and rock music is blaring while the ground crews finish. Everybody is looking up to the announcing booth where the freshman coach is hunched over. You can see Coach Poppers in his blue South Wildcats High School shirt and it's like he's a celebrity. Bob Hoskins, the varsity coach, is walking the fields, stopping to chat with coaches and players. I am at the Olympics, man.

The stands are already full. I guess parents made a point of getting there early for front row seats. Mom has us catch a pop-up, then react to a bunt grounder before running in. She takes the throws and some of the guys screw up easy grounders. Then I see Eric walking across the field in his red-and-white Tri City uniform.

"Hey, beano," he says, swinging down his bat bag.

"Hey," I mutter.

"Listen," he says. "It's already been settled. I'm going to be the starting pitcher for the freshman team and Roy Jackson is going to be the B team pitcher. But we need a good catcher," he continues, nodding to me. "You should try out for it."

It's like he's the coach and offering me a position.

"Yeah, right," I say, turning away.

Eric grabs my shoulder and his eyes change.

"Look. We probably won't play each other because your team sucks and you'll get eliminated. But if we do, man, you really don't want to pitch against me. First of all *I'm* the pitcher," he declares, pounding his chest. "Coach Poppers already told me, so do yourself a favor and go for catcher." He picks up his bat bag. "Because if I go against you, I'll wipe the floor with your sorry ass and you won't make the team at all. It will be bye-bye, beano."

"Don't call me that!" I shout.

My heart is going *boom boom boom.* I stare at him and it's like we are back in the lunchroom and he's dangling that cupcake over his mouth. I have the plastic knife and I'm not sure what I'm going to do. Eric stands there with his mouth open. He shrugs with this fake laugh.

"Hey, whatever. I was just trying to help you, *beano.* But I can see you're too stupid to understand what I'm telling you." He slips the bat bag on his back. "Maybe you can be the water boy or you can cut the lawn before we play. You're good at cutting lawns, right?"

I want to kill him, man. I want to take a bat and cave in his skull. But that's the thing: When you are really angry, you kind of freeze up. And being angry is really bad for your pitching, which Eric knows.

But I just stand there while he laughs and walks away.

Guys like Eric always seem to get the last laugh.

31

WE WON OUR FIRST GAME. Yeah. A forfeit! The other team couldn't field a team because a bunch of kids got the flu and so we got the advantage. The tournament schedule called for two games on Saturday with one game on Sunday. If we won both of our games and Tri City won their games we would meet in a championship game on Sunday.

Well, maybe you've heard about *the Fan*. Cubs are just five outs away from the World Series. It's game six of the National League Championship and a Marlins batter chips it off to left field and Moisés Alou runs to grab it. The ball is going right to the edge of the stands, but Moisés has it, then this dude grabs the ball. Then the Marlins rally and beat the Cubs eight-three and they go on to win Game Seven and go to the World Series. We lived in Chicago at the time and Mom said the guy (the Fan) had to leave town and go into hiding. I'm telling you this, because during our second game, I'm feeling like I grabbed the ball from Moisés Alou.

See, the second game, now in progress, started badly. The

umpire started calling them tight and the Orioles stopped swinging.

Then I started to pitch wild, and now, as the game continues, I'm still doing that.

The problem is every time I think about the Pitcher, I get mad. I don't want to pick a spot. I don't want to follow through like I'm punching a man. I don't want to throw any of the pitches he showed me. I want to pitch my old way and so I throw them in hard and wild. I try a change-up and that's why I throw the floater this kid blasts for a grand slam. Four runs just like that.

That's when Mom comes out, trailing dust with her Oakleys covering her eye that's still black and blue. She walks up on the mound, her mouth tight, pushing up her glasses to those angry eyes.

"Alright, what's going on?"

"I don't know," I answer, shrugging.

"Yes you do know and I'm going to tell you something," she says, leaning forward. "Forget about that asshole in his garage. He's just a drunk and the sooner you and I realize that the better off we are going to both be." She breathed heavily. "Now. Try and use what he showed you if it works, but more than that, pitch the way you know how. Use the ability God gave you. Take your breath, *relax*, push everything out of your mind. The same way we practiced doing homework. *Concentrate.*" She puts her hands on my shoulders. "You can do this, Ricky."

"I don't want to use what he showed me," I grumble.

"Then don't! Pitch it however you want, but you just have to forget about him and do the best you can. Think of this as an early tryout."

"This is an early tryout, Mom," I say.

She nods.

"Then all the better. Just throw it in there like you know how."

She gives me a knuckle bump.

"Get him, Zambrano."

Then Mom leaves.

I try to calm down, but it is just no use. Every time I take my breath, I just can't clear my head. I load up the bases again. The coach gives every batter the take sign when he sees I can't hit the corners. People boo. I want to get off the mound because I feel another grand slam coming. Mom finally calls time and pulls me. We walk off the field and nobody claps. We just walk off and you can hear a pin drop. Artie takes over as I hit the bench. I throw my mitt on the ground and Mom picks it up.

"Don't make it worse than it is," she says, handing it to me.

And that's when I feel like the Fan. Yeah, I am feeling sorry for myself.

But I have a reason.

It gets worse.

***

Mom looks at the scoreboard as I pick up my bat and slide off the weight ring. It's two away and bottom of the sixth and we are chasing three. We had two base hits and then lost gas with two pop-ups. So now I'm up to bat with two on. It's up to me to bring us home and take the lead. I swing my Titanium Slugger around a few times. I like a big bat because of the power. I spit on my gloves and step to the plate, extending my bat to the pitcher, then hoist it to my shoulder.

A new pitcher has come to the mound and he's a real skinny dude who has this crazy windup. I watch his warm-up pitches that are nothing special. Mom looks at me and calls out in a low voice, "Don't go after the garbage, Ricky. Make him give you a good pitch." She's talking nothing high or low. Don't swat at flies and don't dig up anything from the ground.

I step out and tap the rubber and take a couple more swings. The bat fans the air like an airplane propeller making the *whooonh* sound each time. I step back into the box and the umpire guns his finger and hunches down. I stare down the pitcher as he leans forward. He goes back to his set and pitches from the stretch. I swing as the baseball ducks the bat, *whooonh,* then falls into the catcher's mitt. A knuckle ball! They don't act like anything you've seen on the planet. They float in their own weird space and dodge and weave and somehow end up in the catcher's mitt.

"STEEEERIKE!"

I frown at the umpire. Did he really have to yell like that?

The Oriole side is up on the fence and going crazy.

"WAY TO PITCH! NICE ONE JUST LIKE THAT!"

I look toward my side where the Marauders are like, *Go, Ricky, You Can Do It. Make him Work for it. Don't swat at flies.* I bang the plate with my bat and take some more swings. The skinny kid tugs on his hat. He's leaning forward and shaking off the signals. I hold up my hand and snatch up some dirt. I swing again and step back into the batter's box, then snug my cleats into the dirt. I hoist the bat to my shoulder, rotating like it's alive.

The skinny kid shakes off three more signals. I can hear the crowd. The catcher punches his mitt. The ump grunts as he leans down. The kid raises his leg and comes forward. The ball floats toward me like an alien ship. The ball hovers weirdly, but this time I see it and bring my bat around.

Whoonh!

"STEEERIKE!"

Everybody is going crazy and this kid is spitting like he's Roger Clemens. He takes the ball back and grins at me. I really hate it when the pitcher taunts you.

"C'mon, Ricky ... knock it out of the park!"

"You can do it, Ricky!"

"Send this guy home, Ricky!"

The Oriole side is yelling out.

"JUST LIKE THAT, BILLY!"

"YOU GOT HIM, BILLY!"

"ONE MORE, BILLY!"

A skinny kid named *Billy* is going to strike me out? I don't think so. I beat the plate with my bat again and step away and the kid is grinning. Like *he knows* he has me. Two knuckle balls. I should have lit the second one up and blasted it away. I brush back some dirt from the plate with my cleat, then snug in again. The kid is sizing me up, trying to figure out if I'll go for it again.

"Get him, Ricky!"

"You can do it!"

"Blast it out of the park!"

"Protect, Ricky! Protect!"

"Ready batter?"

Some more dirt on the bat and some more spit on the gloves. I hold up my hand, then look at Blue and nod. I bring the bat up, moving it again, and the skinny pitcher leans forward. This time I'm going to make him eat that grin, man. There is no way he is going to float that funky pitch by me again.

He leans back for his set. I breathe in, gripping the bat with my eyes locked on him. *Bring it. Bring it so I can blast if out of the park.* I can see the high school team out there like the moon over the back fence. The kid breaks and comes from the stretch again. I watch his arm come over the top and I cock my shoulder. I have a zero–and–two count and he could throw me a ball, but he doesn't. He's that sure of himself and I watch that knuckle ball lob under the lights like the moon.

I have him now.

I twist back with everything I have and swing as hard as I can.

"Steeerike Three!"

32

AFTER GAMES WE GO TO McDonald's or Dairy Queen. Everybody is usually there from the field and we sit there eating fries and burgers and drinking shakes while talking over the game. I don't know what it is about being in a ball field that makes you so hungry. Maybe the food just tastes better after being outside. I know it's junk food, but Mom and I have had some of our best times under the golden arches. She always has a Diet Coke and plain hamburger, which drives the dude with the headset crazy. *Plain? You want a plain burger?* And then we have to wait and everyone behind us has to wait. And even if we lose, that junk food does make you feel better. But this time it does nothing and thing is ...

We won!

After I struck out, the knuckleballer tried the same thing the next inning. Mom had everyone crowd the plate and he started loading the bases. Then Ronnie hit a home run. That was the game. I thought we would play on Sunday, but now we have a day off before we play Tri City on Monday. When we reach home we both look over to the garage. It's like we can't help ourselves.

"Forget about that asshole," Mom says, getting out of the car.

It's official. The Pitcher had become *that asshole*. But it's not so easy for me to think that way, you know. I blamed him for almost blowing the game. I blamed him for never showing me a change-up and that's why I threw the blooper that resulted in the grand slam. I know that isn't fair. I think I really just felt abandoned. It was weird, man ... when I saw him lying in his bed passed out, I felt like crying. I never felt that way with Fernando.

I want to tell you something: Homework and me don't get along. We just play at different ends of the field. Homework lays there and wants to be done and I want to surf the net, watch ESPN, do just about anything else. But homework just waits for me. Mom walks into the living room. ESPN is doing a roundup of teams in contention for the National League and I'm eating a bowl of Ramen Noodles. Then a bowl of ice cream. Pop Tarts. Cookies. Potato chips. I'm having my *after game* feast after McDonald's that leads to a snooze on the couch. Like I said, something about being in a ball field makes me really hungry.

Mom stands behind the couch seeing my socks and hat on the floor. I can feel it coming, man. I have violated like ten mom-rules.

"You going to clean up this mess?" she asks, staring at my bowls.

"Sure."

"Hmm." Mom's eyes are on the prowl and she's hooking up with her main man, *homework*. They are in cahoots on this one. She throws out the bait.

"How are the books going with that summer reading list?"

The summer reading list: *Catcher in the Rye, There Are*

No Children Here, To Kill a Mockingbird, Precious, Burned.
It goes on and on and I haven't cracked one. I keep meaning
to go the library and get one of the books. That's the thing with
me; I will do anything *but homework*. It's like I'm allergic to it
or something. So I stop in mid-ice-cream with the spoon just
below my mouth. Careful now, there's always a catch. I don't
even know where the list is anymore—maybe on the floor of my
closet.

So I go into lie mode.

"Oh ... good," I answer slowly.

"You have been checking them out of the library?" Mom
continues, raising her eyebrows.

Now I know *homework* is trying to trap me again. So I
consider her question. Mom is just standing there like no
big deal. I see no hazard lights; no warnings like ... *don't say
anything*. Alright, I lie about my homework sometimes. Hey,
man, you got to or you'll always be in the doghouse. It's like one
of my many flaws, you know.

So I just shrug and nod. "Uh huh," I mumble.

Mom crosses her arms with the sparks in her eyes. I know
then I have been played. The question is, how bad.

"The library just sent us a notice," Mom says lightly.

I look up at her, raising my eyebrows.

"Oh ... Yeah?"

"Yeah ..." Mom stands right in front of me. "Seems our
library card was canceled in *June!*"

Just like that she drops me. What a setup, man. I mean,
that's not really fair. She just let me go down the path and then
capped me with a mom-bullet. I drop my bowl of ice cream to
the floor, which just makes things worse. Mom's eyes start flying
around like trapped birds, her chin bobbing.

"Why do you *lie* to me, Ricky? You haven't read one book,
have you?"

"Oh, so you have been spying on me!"

"I should spy on you the way you lie about your homework!"

Now I have something to build around. If I was in a war she would have just given me a foxhole to hide in. I jump up.

"So you're calling me a liar?"

"You are a liar when you *lie!*"

I swing my arms around and start shouting. I learned this trick long ago. Lose your shit and people back off. Some of them.

"How do you expect me to do homework when I'm playing baseball?"

"I expect you to do your homework. *Period.* Do you know how hard I have worked to keep you in school, Ricky? Do you know everything I am doing for you?"

"Well obviously you don't do enough because I still suck," I shout, making no sense at all. But that's the way I roll when I'm cornered. "And it's your fault the Pitcher won't coach me anymore!"

Mom's mouth drops open. Let me just say here, man, I don't know what I'm saying when I fight with Mom. But it has to be *somebody's* fault, because bad things don't just happen for no reason. So I blame her, which is really sick, but I'm in a bad way, you know.

"My fault?" she cries out.

"Yeah ... he was my coach and you ... you turned him into *your boyfriend!*"

"I did nothing of the kind!"

"Yeah, you did," I continue, nodding. "You're so lonely and all, you probably freaked him out and that made him drink again!"

Mom is like blown away. But with me, man, nothing is off-limits and maybe I do think Mom freaked him out. Why would he just start drinking again? I know it's unfair, but that's the way I think, man.

Mom comes close, jabbing her finger.

"You little shit. Don't you lay that on me!" she screams. "He was a drunk before I ever came along and the fact is you never worked hard enough, Ricky! If he doesn't want to coach you then you can't blame me ... why don't you look at yourself!"

I feel my face get hot. I stare at her.

"What are you saying, Mom?"

"I'm saying that you are *lazy*, Ricky. Even with a major league pitcher you haven't gotten control of your pitching because you won't work! You lay around watching ESPN and dream about being a pitcher, but I don't see you working at it. Not the way you should."

I'm seeing red with my heart beating fast, man.

"And that's my fault?"

"Who else's would it be?"

Oh man, I feel like I am on fire. I hate being called lazy. A teacher once called me lazy and I went psycho and ended up in the principal's office. I don't know what it is, but I can't stand it.

"I'M NOT ... LAZY!"

"Yes, you are," Mom says calmly. "You won't do your homework. You won't practice your pitching. You won't do anything! It's no wonder you can't pitch!"

I glare at her, because I'm bleeding now. My eyes flood over and I yell, "I really hate you! You screwed up your life and now you are ruining mine! You're a loser, Mom! You think *I'm* a loser, but that's why Fernando left you because you *bitched at him* all the time and—"

Smack!

I see stars, man. I really do and it's like I can feel her hand on my cheek still. I didn't know getting slapped could hurt so much. But I think Mom is as shocked as I am. We both stare at each other and then we both start crying. But I'm not finished, man.

I glare at her and shout, "You drive everybody away and when I leave I'll never come back here either!"

Then I stomp out of the house and slam the front door.

"Bitch, man. Bitch!"

I stand outside in the heat for a while, trying to cool off. But I can't stop crying, you know. The Pitcher's garage door is all the way down and I don't see Shortstop anywhere. I stare at his garage closed off against the world and I just feel more alone. I sit down on the drive and put my head down on my knees.

Sometimes, man, life just sucks.

33

Grandma arrives the next morning. Mom sets her up in the living room on our pull out couch, which ends up being my bed because Grandma has a bad back. Mom says Grandma believes the Mexicans are going to be rounded up and sent back. I have heard people on television saying they should send back the illegal Mexicans. Mom says our rights are in danger. She says people like Mrs. Payne blame us for taking jobs away from Americans. I don't know, man. I don't see a lot of people wanting to cut lawns and lay sod, you know.

Anyway, I should tell you: Mom and I don't say anything to Grandma about our fight. I mean, Mom never slapped me before and I think we both freaked. Last night, after we had it out, I sat by her on the couch and we watched that movie *The Blind Side* again. It's pretty cool the way this guy from the projects gets taken in by a rich family, man, and makes it to the NFL. And the movie has a happy ending, and Mom and I dug that. She rubbed my hair and I leaned against her and she murmured she was sorry. I said I'm sorry too. And then we watched this dude overcome the odds and make it to the pros and end up with Sandra Bullock as his mom.

She's a pretty good-looking mom. But so is mine.

Anyway, Sunday, the day Grandma comes, is crazy hot. The sidewalks are so hot you can fry an egg. Joey did it once. It sizzled and burned. The next day it was still there, all rubbery and brown.

Joey and I throw the ball in the street while Shortstop snoozes in the shade and makes these whimpering sounds. The Pitcher has his garage up just enough to see his ankles.

Mom is on the porch smoking a cigarette and staring at his house. Then she crosses the street and knocks on the garage. The garage goes up and the Pitcher stands there. They start shouting and I can hear it all the way across the street.

"You're just a drunk feeling sorry ... ."

"That's my business ... ."

"He needs you ... ."

"I'm sorry ... that's just not who I am ... ."

Then the garage rolls back down. I see Mom talking to the door, but the garage never goes back up. Then she comes back across the street with her eyes wet. Mom doesn't say a word. It is like everything good has ended and something really bad is on the way. You can just feel it.

Joey leaves, and I start throwing a tennis ball against our garage. I catch it on the hop in the heat-cooling street.

Kaboomp! Kaboomp!

OK. So I don't have a coach anymore.

Kaboomp! Kaboomp!

OK. So the Pitcher isn't going with us tomorrow.

Kaboomp! Kaboomp!

OK. So Eric will probably wipe the field with me.

Kaboomp! Kaboomp!

OK. My pitching has gone crazy and I have no idea why.

Kaboomp! Kaboomp!
Why won't he at least talk to Mom?
Kaboomp! Kaboomp!
Kaboomp! Kaboomp!
Kaboomp!
KAPOW!

I watch the ball take a weird hop over my head and *bump bump bump* up the Pitcher's drive and under the garage. Shortstop watches it vanish under the garage and turns to me like, *Well? Are you going to get it?* I stare at the dark gap and don't really want to go after it. I have been thinking a lot about what Mom said, you know—that the reason the Pitcher left was because of me. Maybe I do suck that bad.

So I cross the hot street with the ballgame hissing like some kind of demon. I walk up the drive and can feel my heart bumping when the door clanks up and the Pitcher is standing there. He squints down at me with the green tennis ball in his hand and a cigarette in the other. He has this wrinkly Hawaiian shirt on that looks like he's slept in it. Dark half-moons are under his eyes and he coughs a couple times, then holds up the ball.

"What the hell are you playing with a goddamn tennis ball for?"

"It bounces better."

He spits off to the side.

"That ain't going to help your pitching," he mutters, tossing the ball to me.

Then he walks back in his garage. I hesitate, then follow him into the tobacco-stinking darkness still holding my glove. The Pitcher groans down into his chair and lights another cigarette, holding it by his cheek . His hand is shaking and he coughs some more. I stand behind him in his La-Z-Boy while he drinks his beer.

"I heard you pitched lousy," he says without turning around.

I shrug.

"Yeah."

He shakes his head.

"Still can't get it together, huh, rockhead?"

"Guess not."

"You got the talent, boy, but you ain't got the drive."

He taps his cigarette again and keeps his eyes on the game. I step forward and squint at the back of his head.

"How come you put the garage down on my mom?"

The Pitcher sips his beer again.

"Why couldn't you throw a goddamn decent pitch?"

"I don't know—"

"Bullshit. You just don't do the work."

I stare at him watching the game.

"How come you started drinking again?"

"I drink because I drink."

Smoke rolls up above his head. I look at the photos again that seem dingy now. The fan whirs in the background. The garage seems like a crappy old garage and I'm not sure why that is.

I look at him again.

"You should have opened the door for my mom."

"You want me to be nice to your mom?"

"Yeah."

"Then pitch like I goddamn taught you and stop waiting for your mother to bail your ass out."

He shakes his head as someone knocks one out of the park.

"Gotta pinch those corners," he mutters to the television.

I stare at him, feeling like he has just knocked the wind out of me.

"You don't know what it's like," I mumble.

"What?"

The Pitcher turns around.

"You talking about that dyslexia shit?"

"Yeah."

He motions me forward, like a wizard.

"Come here, you rockhead."

I walk up slowly and he picks up a pen. There is a crossword puzzle in the *Jacksonville Chronicle* with half the words filled in. "Now watch closely," he says, taking the pen and drawing a baseball. "What am I doing?"

"Drawing a baseball."

"That's right, rockhead." The Pitcher looks at me, his eyes bloodshot and yellow. "But what hand am I drawing with?"

He holds up his hand with the pen. I stare, then turn and look at the picture on the wall. I can hear the fan and the television. He has his leg up, looking over his shoulder, his eyes pinned to the batter. The Pitcher is ready to deliver all that *southpaw* fury.

"Your right hand," I whisper.

"That's right," he says. "When I was your age I played on the high school team and pitched righty. Then like a rockhead I rode a motorcycle and wrecked my arm. They put me in a cast and put pins in my shoulder," he continues, leaning back. "When they took it off, I couldn't pitch no more."

"So what did you do?"

"Whaddaya think? I decided I was going to pitch anyway and would do it with my left arm. Coach said it would never work. So I told him I would see him in the spring tryouts."

The Pitcher turns back to the television and pulls on his cigarette.

"So ... so what happened then?"

He nods across the room.

"I filled up that bucket with rocks and started throwing. I threw rocks at everything—birds, trees, gulls. I threw rocks until I thought my arm would fall off and then I started to pitch. I didn't have no speed and no accuracy." The Pitcher turns, his eyes piercing the gloomy garage. "But nobody was going to keep me off that goddamn mound. Not the coach. Not the doctors. That's when I picked up my nickname."

I look at him.

"Rockhead?"

"Yeah." He turns, pointing his cigarette. "But *nobody* was going to tell me I couldn't pitch. You understand that, *rockhead?*"

He turns back to the television and sips his beer.

"Your problem is you want it, but you don't want it bad enough. I don't care if you have mush up there in your noggin. You have an arm, but if you don't overcome your problems, it ain't worth a nickel. You gotta do the work."

"I do the work," I mutter.

He shakes his head.

"Nah ... you don't. But I'll bet you that Payne kid does the work," he says, looking over. "I'll bet he don't let anything stop him."

"He's had every lesson in the world!" I cry out.

"Yeah and you had a major league pitcher coaching you, so what's your excuse now?" he says, looking at me.

I stand there, not moving. The Pitcher flicks his cigarette at the television.

"How'd your mother do coaching?"

I shrug. "Alright. We won ... but she was upset because you didn't come."

"Yeah ... well," he says, moving his legs. "I ain't nobody's idea of a boyfriend. I would have been just fine if *you people* had not come knocking on my garage."

I hear the *you people* like I hear wetback. It echoes all over the garage and I stand up. The same hot sweaty feeling breaks out on my forehead. I stand there, feeling the rage roll in like waves. And maybe that's why I say what I say next. Sometimes I'm like those volcanoes with red fire that spouts up.

"At least I'm not sitting in a garage and drinking beer all day and feeling sorry for myself."

The Pitcher points to the door with his cigarette.

"Get the hell out of my goddamn garage!"

I don't move and he stands up.

"Go! Get the hell out of here!"

I pick up my mitt. I can barely walk and I stumble across his garage. My heart is pounding as I turn around at the door.

"I don't need you!" I yell. "I don't need someone who treats people *like shit!*"

The Pitcher just stares at me. I walk out then and hear the garage go down behind me. I don't give a care anymore. I keep on walking to my house, then sit down on the porch and don't move. I don't hear his television. I don't hear anything except my own sniffling. I stay outside with my head down on my knees. I stay there until my chest stops heaving.

It takes a while.

34

I TAKE MOM'S LAPTOP AND sit in the darkness of my room and play the YouTube clip of Jack Langford throwing the final pitch in the '78 World Series. I watch him jump into his catcher's arm after the batter pops up. The catcher stands there and waits for the ball to come down and then he makes the catch and the Pitcher comes flying in and jumps on him. He just won the World Series. He just won the biggest game in the world. The other players pile on and you can't see the Pitcher anymore.

And I look for him to emerge, you know. Like where did that guy go and who was the guy in the garage drinking beer and watching television? Where did all that greatness go? I just keep playing that clip over and over, looking for clues.

I must have drifted off because I wake up and it's like five AM and Grandma is in my room. She is screaming in Spanish and I'm hearing all this while I'm half-asleep.

"Calm down, Grandma. Calm down," I say groggily. "What are you trying to say?"

"Your mother is sick!" she shouts, grabbing my hand.

That's when I get chilled like when you see a squashed cat in the road. Grandma pulls me into Mom's bedroom where she's sitting. Blood spreads out like a red sea behind her. She looks up woozily and tries to smile, but she's really, really pale. I mean pale like when I walked up to my aunt with her arms crossed. Dead pale.

"Mom ... you're bleeding!" I cry out.

"I'm fine. I'm fine," she murmurs, moving unsteadily. "Go ... go back to bed, Ricky."

But she isn't fine. She looks like she might faint. I stare at the bloodstain that looks like an ocean to me and I start thinking about the things I should be doing. All the stuff they tell you on television to do in an emergency. *Dial 9-1-1! Dial 9-1-1! Dial 9-1-1!* But it's like everything is in slow motion and all I do is stare.

"Mom ... you're bleeding!"

"I'm fine ... Ricky," Mom repeats, but she is wavering. "Just a little."

Grandma starts chattering in Spanish and Mom looks at me with this helpless hollow expression. That's when I take off out the door. I am in fight or flight mode or whatever they call it. I run into the street in my pajamas. The moon is out and the whole world is blue and the road is still warm.

I run up to the Pitcher's garage and start banging and screaming.

"JACK! JACK! JACK!"

I like never call him Jack, but I'm banging on the garage with my fists and the springs or the coils are clanging. I throw my body against the garage and then the door starts moving up. The Pitcher staggers out of the darkness in a white T-shirt and shorts.

"What the hell are you banging on—?"

"Mom's bleeding!" I swallow. *"She's bleeding to death!"*

The Pitcher stares at me, then he runs. I have never seen an older dude run in bare feet before. He runs across the street into the house and straight back to the bedroom. The Pitcher busts into the room and sees Mom and the blood on the sheet, then grabs up the phone by her bed.

"I'm calling 9-1-1," he says, looking down at her.

Mom holds up her hand.

"No, don't ... I'll be fine," she says weakly.

The Pitcher stares at her with the phone in his hand. He's really big in her bedroom in his white T-shirt with his hair on his forehead and I'm praying he won't listen to Mom. There are times she doesn't make sense and this is one of those times. He frowns and shakes his head.

"You're goddamn hemorrhaging, Maria!"

Mom holds up her hands, but she's having trouble sitting up.

"No ... no ... I'll be fine. Just don't call the doctor," she pleads.

The Pitcher stares at her like she's lost her mind.

"You have to go the hospital," he says, shaking his head.

"I don't want to go to the hospital."

"Maria ... I either call the goddamn ambulance or I drive you to the goddamn hospital," he tells her, holding the phone against his chest.

Mom looks down and I see her eyes go to the blood.

"No ambulance," she says in a small voice.

The Pitcher drops the phone.

"Let's go then."

He starts to help Mom up and then she just collapses, like she *swoons*. I mean straight down to the floor. The Pitcher scoops her up like a princess and she passes out in his arms.

"Let's go," he shouts and we leave the house and then I'm opening the door to his station wagon. He puts Mom in the front and jumps in the driver's side. The Pitcher doesn't even have his shoes, but he pulls the keys up from under the mat and looks at me.

"Stay with your grandmother. I'll call you from the hospital."

And then he just tears down the road with Mom passed out against him. I stare at his blue exhaust rolling under the moon and watch his taillights disappear. And then it's just quiet, man. I mean *really* quiet. I stand out there in the street and start crying, because nobody can lose that much blood. You just don't have enough, you know. I wipe my eyes and now I'm shivering. I can't stop my teeth from *chachachachachachattering!*

Grandma is on the couch clutching her rosary beads and has a little cross on the coffee table. She is saying devotions or something to Mary or whoever. We never really went to church. I know I said we did, but we only go on Christmas. Mom said God could hear us without going to church. But I wish we had gone. I guess that's the way it is with God. You don't want him until *you really need* him and we really need him now.

I sit down next to Grandma and she keeps her head bowed and keeps praying. I stare at the little plastic cross and then I get down on my knees. I start praying and asking God to let Mom stay. I promise I'll do my homework and I won't swear and I'll quit raising hell at school. I promise I'll do anything. No more cussing or throwing stuff under the Pitcher's garage or giving Mom hell or lying about my homework. I'll do whatever He wants.

Just let Mom stay.

35

I'M IN THE WAITING ROOM and I'm nervous, man. I hate hospitals. Maybe everybody does. To me it's where people go to get operated on and die. Sorry. That's the way I see it. I watch the television shows and whenever someone is in the hospital then that's it. The Pitcher had come back to get me and Grandma. He drove like the wind through the empty streets and now we are sitting in this brightly lit room. Everyone looks like they just woke up and ambulances are coming in, wheeling people through with oxygen masks.

Scary shit, man.

We see this Indian doctor with her hair pinned back and a loose dress thing on. It might be Mom's doctor. I'm not sure. I haven't been sure of anything since they took Mom away on a gurney. I watch other people come into the emergency room. People slump in the corners on the red couches; a few people doze. I think of myself in flip flops and shorts and my red pajama shirt. The Pitcher tries to smooth down his hair, then gives up and stares at his hands. At least he has on his old crappy loafers and I wonder when he realized he didn't have shoes. I think of the way he looked when he picked Mom up and ran for his car.

It was like he was running for *his life.*

Grandma sits in the corner of the emergency room with her rosary. She's like chanting to herself and nobody bothers the little old Mexican lady muttering away. Nobody cares about anything when you are in a hospital, man. The only thing people care about is getting the hell out of there. The Indian doctor pushes through the double doors in her white coat.

"Are you Ricky?" she asks, looking at me.

Now, I'm freaking.

"Yeah ... Yeah ... I'm Ricky," I answer.

The Indian doctor smiles, but it's one of those smiles teachers give you right before they tell you the bad news. Not good, man.

"We talked on the phone."

"Yeah ... right," I mumble.

She holds out her hand to the Pitcher.

"And you are Mr. Langford?"

"Yes ma'am."

I never heard that before. Dr. Aziz sits down on the couch and we huddle close like she has a big secret. Grandma stays in the corner. I guess she figures she could do more talking to the Big Man.

"Maria wanted me to talk to you and asked that you bring some things for her," she begins, looking at the Pitcher.

"I can do that," he says.

The doctor has dark circles under her eyes and she pauses.

"Maria is resting and we have stopped the hemorrhaging for now," she says slowly, looking at both of us. "But she is very sick."

My heart does not like this and I feel like bolting out the door. The Pitcher sits with his eyes focused like he's on the mound.

"We have to run a lot of tests, but her kidneys are failing. The lupus has attacked her internal organs, but we just don't know to what extent," she continues looking at the Pitcher, then me. "The first thing we have to do is get her blood levels straight and ..."

To tell you the truth, man, I start to space out. I hear the medical speak and try to pay attention except my mind keeps jumping ahead. *So she is going to die. So she is going to die.* But I nod and say *uh huh I see, yes, ok, uh huh* and try to look like you're supposed to look. When people tell me bad things I sort of go somewhere else. So I look like I am listening, but I don't hear a word the doctor is saying.

Her eyes flatten out into large brown circles.

"I won't lie to you. Maria might have waited too long for us to—"

"You mean too long to get well?" I interrupt, feeling like I have just been prodded awake. Because that has to be what she means. I'm not even going to the other place. Dr. Aziz looks at me and her eyes soften.

"Well, let's just see how the next twenty-four hours go," she says, looking at the Pitcher again.

"She is on a dialysis machine and we have moved her upstairs for now."

I see. Yes. Alright. Hmm, Uh huh. I think I said that. At least that's what *I think.* I mean on the television shows everyone gets bad news and looks real calm. Except the ladies who throw themselves on the floor going *NO, NO, NO.* But I'm not going to do that. The Pitcher, he just keeps nodding with the hawk eyes. I figure if he can be cool, then I can too.

"She keeps talking about a baseball game, but of course she can't participate," the doctor continues, looking at the Pitcher and me. "I don't understand her preoccupation with this game when she is very ill." Dr. Aziz shakes her head. "She knew how sick she was but didn't tell anyone."

I nod like a puppet, keeping my hands clasped in the right position. What I want to do is tell that doctor all about Mom. She just doesn't know the way Mom worked with me every day in the street. The way she read from books to try and teach me how to pitch. Or how she got me *Hooked on Phonics* when I couldn't read. She doesn't know about the way she would hold up these flash cards because I just couldn't remember eight times seven is fifty-six or nine times eight is seventy-two. Like how we sat on our porch every day with those cards, man. She didn't know anything about her being my coach on every team I joined.

All she sees is the questions, you know.

I want to say to her: *Did I tell you she got a World Series pitcher to coach me? I'm not so good at school and we are working on that too. But she told me I could do whatever I wanted because I have this dream of being a major league pitcher. That's why she got me the dude sitting right here; World Series pitcher man! 1978 against the Cardinals. Bet you never had that in here before! But first I have to make the high school team and Mom is all about that. She said I'm going to make it and I will. So that's the plan and we are all on board. So don't let her slip away. I need her, man, don't let her slip away."*

"Ricky?"

Dr. Aziz is staring at me. I'm doing a great job, man, of keeping it together. She is probably like, damn, this little dude is tough! And I am, man. I can take a lot, you know. I mean, I feel like being one of those ladies on TV, but like men don't cry, you know, in front of people. And it is time to be a man now, right?

So I look at her real steady-eyed.

"Yeah...what up," I say calmly.

The doctor's eyes get real sad and she takes my hand, which is kind of weird, but that's when I see this red table, man. It's like got *People* magazine and *Good Housekeeping* and these women's magazines all over it. But the thing I'm staring at is the rain. Something must be leaking from the ceiling, because there's a lot of rain on that table. And Dr. Aziz is just staring at me like I'm bawling or something. But I'm keeping it together. I'm telling you straight.

Even though the rain, man, it just keeps coming down.

36

MOM AND I ARE IN a space shuttle except it's more like a fighter jet. We are going past planets and shooting across the universe with a million stars around us. *That one looks good, Ricky,* she says, squeezing my shoulder. *Oh, that's Jupiter, Mom, let's keep going.* So we go by like Mars and Uranus and Neptune and I'm guiding this rocket ship and Mom is saying, *You find us a good planet to live on, Ricky. I know you can do it.* The music is like Kanye West's long synthesizer rip at the end of that one song *Runaway.* Then I see this green-and-blue planet. *Hey, Mom, that looks like a good one. I think it's Earth.* And then I don't feel her hand anymore. I turn around and her seat is empty.

Mom!

I look around.

Mom!

I open my eyes and stare at the ceiling in my bedroom. You know how it is after a big bang? Like a firecracker or one of those cherry bombs Joey's dad buys from some guy in Mexico that make all the windows rattle. After those things blow up you can't hear a thing, man, and it sounds like the whole world is taking a breath. That's the way it is in the house. I figure I'll get up and Mom will be there eating her toast with her coffee and reading the *Jacksonville Chronicle*. She'll look up and smile in her Hawaiian robe.

"How did you sleep, Ricky?"

"Good," I'll answer, yawning.

"Are you hungry?"

"No. Not really," I'll mumble, slumping down at our breakfast bar.

"Get yourself some cereal," she'll say, nodding to the cabinets.

Or she'll get up and make pancakes like she does every weekend. And maybe we will eat on the patio, which is cool because you feel rich eating outside. I don't know why, but you can just imagine rich people doing that. Then we will talk around the patio table and I will rip on Dr. Freedom and make Mom laugh or imitate Coach Devin and Mrs. Payne. Then we'll go throw the ball in the street and work on my pitching.

So I figure Mom will be there in her robe and our day will pass just like any other. But then I hear the snoring. Mom snores like an animal, which is almost like a small motor. This snoring shakes the house. And then it breaks into this snorting like some kind of wild beast. I get up and walk out of my bedroom and see the Pitcher on our couch with his feet hanging off. His mouth is open with his cigarettes and a can of Good Times on the floor.

But now I don't see him.

I see Mom.

The machines are breathing and there's one showing her heartbeat like PAC-MAN that Mom likes to play where the yellow dot eats white dots before they turn into blue monsters and eat you. And that's what I'm seeing now, man—lots of blue monsters that are going to eat Mom through all these tubes. I don't know what to do, so I just stand there with the Pitcher. He looks freaked too and then Mom opens her eyes a little.

"Hey, Ricky," she says real softly.

She holds out her hand and it feels rough from playing ball. She doesn't really close her hand, just leaves it there. I close mine, because I don't care how many tubes they have going into her, I'm going to hang on. She has her eyes closed again and then she speaks with her mouth barely moving.

"You have your big game tomorrow."

"I'm not going."

She opens her eyes.

"Don't give me that bullshit. You are going, Ricky," she says in a stronger voice. "It's what we have been working toward ..."

"But who's going to coach us?"

"I'll coach the team," the Pitcher says then. "Until your mom gets better."

I stare at the Pitcher and he nods. But to my way of thinking, man, I'm done with baseball. This all happened because of me playing baseball. I shake my head, looking down.

"I'm not playing, Mom."

Her eyes get fierce.

"You have to play, Ricky! The freshman coaches will be watching." Mom pauses and I can tell just talking is taking her strength. "It's your moment to shine."

Moment to shine, man, I have heard that before. And now I am seeing all the way back to when my kindergarten teacher said I couldn't remember my lines for the Christmas play. Mom just stood there and said she would make sure I knew them. The teacher shook her head. "I'm sorry, Ms. Hernandez, but I think we might have to use someone else." Mom stared at her, her eyes moving, her chin bobbing. "No. He has to have his moment to shine."

And that was that.

Mom's hand gets real loose and she's breathing heavily. She

falls sleep again and I hate to say it, but I cry all over her bed. I cry with my head down on the mattress until the Pitcher drives me home. Grandma helps me to bed. But now I'm staring at the Pitcher on the couch. An ESPN announcer drones on about Michael Vick's return to football. I walk over and turn off the television and that's when he wakes up. Actually, I lied. I go and look in Mom's room and see the dark stain on her bed and then run back out and punch his arm.

"Where's Mom?"

The Pitcher sits up and coughs.

"Argh ..." I think he says at first. "She's at the hospital," he answers hoarsely.

"Where's my mom?" I repeat.

The Pitcher picks up his cigarettes.

"Your mom is still at the hospital. We took her ... remember?"

He then hocks these really gross things into his Good Times. The dude must travel with spares. I wait and don't say anything about him coming back to pick up some things for Mom. When people take a suitcase to the hospital, it's a bad sign. I know this because the Pitcher talked to somebody on the phone and said the same thing happened with his wife. He had taken her a suitcase of clothes and makeup and books and toiletries and *she never left.*

"She's doing fine," he says, standing up with pillow marks in his cheek. He groans and holds his back, wincing. "Shit ... that couch is full of rocks."

"She's not coming back, is she?"

He winces again, rubbing his back.

"Don't be a rockhead; of course she's coming back." The Pitcher stretches. "Don't ever get old," he mutters, walking like a cripple toward the kitchen. "Let's get you something to eat."

There is no way I can eat with all the butterflies in my stomach. That's what Mom called them. She said it was normal to have butterflies before a game or a big test or having to stand up and give a speech in class. But these are butterflies of dread, man. This is not the good kind of nervousness that Mom said made you better. Right now it's making me feel like I am going to throw up.

"I don't want to eat anything."

The Pitcher turns around with bloodshot eyes.

"Don't be stupid. This is the championship, right?"

"I'm not playing,"

I decide right then I'm not playing. Not with Mom in the hospital about to float off anytime. No way. Baseball did this to her so *screw baseball*. I just want to go back to the hospital and make sure she is still there. I face the Pitcher and cross my arms.

"I want to go see my *Mom!*"

"You can't. She's sleeping," he replies, staring into the refrigerator.

I'm suspicious. Maybe he is just holding out with the bad news. Don't tell the kid, you know. I stare at him closely and my heart is really acting weird.

"Why can't I see her?"

"We won't make the game then." He holds up his hand. "After the game we'll go see her."

"NO!" I shake my head. "I want to see her now!"

I am acting like a little kid and kind of yelled the last word. The Pitcher looks pretty miserable. He's thinking he could be watching a ballgame, but instead he's stuck with this asshole Mexican kid.

"Look," he begins again. The phone rings and I jump up and grab it.

"Mom ... *Mom!*"

"Hi, honey ...," she says weakly.

"Mom." I breathe in relief and say it again. "*Mom.*"

I had no idea if it was going to be her, but in a way it had to be. She hadn't died while I was asleep. She is still here.

"How are you?"

I start to speak and my throat tightens up. So I start hitting the couch with my fist. I have to do something to keep from blubbering.

"Good ... Mr. Langford is making me some breakfast," I tell her, watching him take out some milk.

"That's good ... he's going to coach you today ... I'll be home soon," she continues in a voice that doesn't sound at all like her.

"I don't want to play, Mom," I say, hitting the couch again. "I want to come see you."

"Do not come to see me! You have a game to play. I want you to play that game, Ricky. I want those coaches to see you. That is the best thing you can do for me. I will get well ... don't worry," she finishes, starting to sound faint again.

"I can't stop worrying, Mom."

"Concentrate on the game. You have a gift, Ricky. Now I want you to show it to the world."

And then she gets real faint again like she is all tired out. I try to stop crying, because I know it is hard on her to hear it. So I keep punching the couch and take a real deep breath.

"Are you going to get well, Mom?"

"Yes ... don't worry ... I just want you to concentrate on the game. Just listen to Mr. Langford."

I'm hitting the couch with my fist.

"Just remember you can do anything you want."

"Yeah, I know, Mom."

"I love you, Ricky."

"I love you too, Mom," I whisper, pushing my mouth against the phone.

Then she is gone. I hold the phone, feeling close to her even with the dial tone. I hang up and stare at the couch. I wipe my eyes and breathe deeply. The Pitcher puts a cigarette in his mouth and talks around it.

"How is she?"

"She didn't sound right," I mutter.

"Nobody sounds right in a goddamn hospital."

I watch him turn and break eggs into a frying pan.

"I'm not hungry," I repeat.

The Pitcher holds the cigarette by his waist and frowns.

"Don't be a rockhead. Rule number one: You eat breakfast. How the hell can you pitch without a breakfast? I always ate two eggs, two pieces of toast, two pieces of bacon and coffee on game days. Some days I ate a goddamn steak and pitched even better. You gotta eat."

I wipe my eyes again. All I want to do is go to the hospital and make sure Mom is still in her bed. I don't want to pitch. I don't want to play baseball. But I also know she wants me to play and that I have to play. She has given everything to get me to this point, so I will play this one game and then beat it to the hospital.

"Alright, I'll eat some cereal," I mumble.

"Cereal!" The Pitcher scowls. "Cereal ain't no food for a pitcher! You gotta eat some goddamn eggs!"

I stare him down.

"I don't like eggs!"

He snorts.

"That's why you're having trouble; you don't eat any eggs. You need protein. You can't go out and pitch on goddamn cereal!"

"I always eat cereal before I pitch."

The Pitcher leans on the counter and points his cigarette at me.

"Yeah ... what did you eat before the last game?"

"Cereal!"

"I rest my case," he says, holding up his hands.

I scowl and glare at him. The Pitcher really pisses me off when he wants to. But I'm not thinking about Mom anymore and maybe that was his play. He starts heating the pan, then breaks two eggs into a bowl.

"Oh like food is going to make me pitch better."

"It might," he murmurs, opening the refrigerator. "You can't pitch any worse."

Man, this dude. I open my mouth to tell him what I really think about his breakfast. He looks at me with his head in the fridge.

"You like bacon and toast, rockhead?"

"No!"

"Good," he says. "We'll have bacon and toast too."

37

THE PITCHER TELLS ME TO get my mitt. The game isn't until four and we are out on the field behind Roland School in the dawn light. The field looks like glass drops from the dew with the infield the color of dark mustard. I had figured we'd rest up for the game, but the Pitcher just shook his head and said, "Got a pitch I want to show you." So now we are on the mound with the wind whipping across, tufting the Pitcher's normally greased hair. He throws away his cigarette with the morning light creasing his craggy cheek.

"Alright. You need this now. I never had one, but you might need this now," he says, holding the ball like a present.

"What? You mean a—"

"You know what I mean. Just shut up and listen, alright?"

So I do.

"Alright ..." He pauses, his eyes locking me in place. "The change-up is all about doing what's not expected," he begins. "The batter figures he's got you, because he knows your fastball.

So you give him the same look and he thinks that fastball is coming again, but the ball comes in ten miles slower, curving, dropping or doing just about anything you can come up with."

The Pitcher nods the ball at me.

"By the time the batter figures out your pitch he's already out in front of it. That's what you want ... you following me?"

"Yeah!"

"Satchel Paige probably had the best change-up in history until they outlawed it. He called it the hesitation pitch." The Pitcher raises his arm. "His arm would pause over the top and then come down. They said everybody had to have a continuous motion after that. But the concept is the same. You want the guy to think you are giving him a straight fastball. That's why it's all in the delivery." The Pitcher holds the ball up. "The batter expects one thing and you do another."

"So you fake him out?"

"Yeah, something like that. Alright now, you gotta use that noggin of yours on this one, because I'm going to give you some technique here. You hold the ball against your palm with your index, middle, and ring finger spread across the seams at the widest point," he explains, gripping the ball. "These fingers are on top of the ball ... see, right here ... while the pinky and thumb are placed underneath. You keep your wrist stiff and exert pressure on the ball with all five fingers."

The Pitcher stretches back and holds the ball over his head. "Go into your windup and remember to pivot and shift your body weight from the back foot forward toward home plate," he continues, bringing the ball over his head. "As you release the pitch, bring the ball down like you are scratching a blackboard. You see. It should look just like your fastball." He stands up and nods. "If you do it right, the ball should start out fast and hit the brakes about fifteen yards out as it drops down on the hitter."

"Yeah, OK," I say.

The Pitcher goes through the motion several times and looks

over.

"Follow through. Your feet should parallel each other at the end of the pitch, and your throwing arm should come across the front of your body. You got it, rockhead?"

"Yeah ... I think so."

His eyes grow serious, beating the ball against his palm. "You gotta hit the mark with this pitch, because if you don't ... they'll knock it over the goddamn fence."

The Pitcher hands me the ball and walks to the plate.

"Alright," he calls out. "Let's see your change-up."

I nod and position the ball in my hand. I get the grip straight in my glove and set myself. I pull in, take my breath, then come over the top. The Pitcher stares at me as the ball lollipops into his glove.

"What the hell was that piece of crap?"

"A change-up!"

"That ain't no change-up!" He throws the ball back. "A chimp could throw a better change-up than that! Get your grip straight and make sure you follow through. Remember to scratch the blackboard at the end of your motion. You throw another blooper like that and the batter will knock your socks off."

I take the ball and reset myself. I get my grip and put the ball toward the back of my hand. I breathe, then come over the top, but my release is too high. The Pitcher catches it and stares at me. He shakes his head.

"Listen, if that's your change-up then you are in trouble," he says, whipping it back. "Remember to put it far back in your hand and scratch the shit out of the blackboard in your delivery. It should look and feel like your fastball."

"Yeah, OK," I mutter, tugging on my hat.

Now I'm beginning to have doubts. Maybe he is right. Maybe a change-up isn't such a good idea. The potential for disaster is really high if I don't throw it right. I throw in pitch after pitch, but they either float like a blooper or just go wild. None of the pitches behave and I have to throw some straight fastballs just to set myself. The Pitcher finally stands up.

"Look, kid. This may not be the pitch for you. With a change-up, it is all or none. You can't go back once you make the change. They see it coming, then you are dead in the water. Remember, it's about *what's not* expected. They gotta to believe you are giving them a fastball."

I nod and my arm is beginning to ache, which isn't good on game day.

"Let me try it one more time," I plead, holding up my mitt.

The Pitcher shrugs and throws the ball back. I set myself on the mound again. He squats down and turns his cap backward.

"See the pitch, Ricky," he says. "See it and remember what I told you. Put the ball far back in your hand and make sure your fingers scratch the blackboard."

I pull in the ball and position it toward the back of my hand. I close my eyes and take my breath, feeling the silence. I open up and come over the top with my fingers scratching the blackboard at the end. The ball comes out like my fastball, but right away I can tell it is different. It moves without rotation like a knuckle ball, then drops straight down. The Pitcher catches it and doesn't move.

He just holds the ball in his mitt, framing it for the world.

38

YOU ARE ALWAYS NERVOUS ON game day. And if you are pitching then it's even worse. Some guys throw up before every game. I would if I tried to put anything in my stomach the hour before the game. It's like my stomach gets tight as a drum and food or drink are out of the question. That drove Mom nuts because she always tried to get me to drink or eat something before games. So it was amazing the Pitcher got me to eat an egg and some bacon, but now my stomach is doubly tight.

We load his station wagon with the catcher equipment, balls, extra bats, clipboards, batting helmets, sunflower seeds, extra socks, gloves, hats, shirts, pants. We both work silently trying not to think about Mom in the hospital. She should be with us and I feel like we are more soldiers than ballplayers. I throw in a folding chair. The Pitcher said his knees gave him hell sometimes from standing.

Then I give him Mom's hat.

"That's your Mom's, kiddo," he says, frowning.

I shrug. "She would want you to wear it."

The Pitcher holds the hat, then adjusts the band and snugs it on.

"How's it look?"

The hat rides high and I grin.

"Good!"

He gives me a look.

"Yeah, right."

The Pitcher drives like he pitches: fast and furious, dodging in and out between lanes like he is taunting a batter. I like his station wagon with the windows open and the air-conditioning on. I like that it is full of cigarettes, newspapers, baseballs, Skoal cans, Good Times cans, a bat, magazines, fast-food wrappers. The Pitcher passes cars and cusses and yells at people who don't get out of his way. We reach the high school like it is yesterday.

We unload in the parking lot. The day is clear and bright like you can see a million miles. We start across the field under a perfect blue sky and I see Eric coming across the infield. He has two bats sticking up on his back like he's going to get in his Maserati and drive away from pitching his first major league game. The Pitcher goes into the dugout as Eric turns with his sunglasses reflecting the world.

"Hey, *beano!* You still playing?"

I ignore him and take out my batting gloves. He stops in front of me with these absurdly white teeth and his uniform starched and perfect. He gnashes his gum, spitting an eraser-colored wad at my feet.

"So, you aren't pitching ... are you?"

"I am," I say, taking out my mitt.

Eric snorts and shoves more gum in his mouth.

"Dude, first of all we are going to wipe the field with you guys," he says, holding up his hands. "I don't know how you guys even got in the championship!"

"Yeah, we'll see," I say, pulling on my gloves.

He laughs and pops a bubble in my face and leans in close.

"Listen. I told you, your only hope is to catch. Both high school coaches are watching this game, dude, and you don't want to show them you can't even get it over the plate, right? I mean you really *suck* at pitching, beano."

I stare at him and for the first time I see his fear.

"Says the guy who doesn't have a fastball."

A smile quivers on his mouth.

"Look, dude, I heard your Mom is sick. I don't think you should be out here playing baseball when your Mom is in the hospital."

I feel my heart rise up. I have no idea how Eric would know this.

"I heard she could die, man, and I sure wouldn't want my last time spent on a baseball field when—"

"Shut up!"

The stupid little smile disappears.

"Hey, it's not my fault your mom is so *desperate* she digs up some loser old pitcher to coach you who I hear is a drunk. Maybe she's getting what she deserved."

I move toward him and Eric drops his bat bag. He holds up his fists and steps back like we are in a ring. I'm seeing blood now.

"Go ahead, beano. Throw a punch," he taunts, his blue eyes goading me. I think about it. Just throw a punch and forget about the game. He smiles again.

"You going to pull out a knife, beano?"

I stare at him and know this is his play.

"You aren't worth it," I mutter, picking up my bat bag.

Eric stares at me, then grins and picks up his bag. The bat antennas go back up and he shakes his head. "You just don't have it, beano. You never did, because you suck at pitching." He pauses, his eyes growing small. "Just don't hit me, beano. You hit me and I'm going to have to kick your ass."

Then he walks away with his two bats and joins the Tri City Team warming up. I feel like someone has just taken away all my strength.

***

Speeches before games are usually pretty corny. Mom would always tell us to try our hardest and have fun out there. On Tri City they had a team prayer led by Gino before each game. This was after the parents signed contracts that said they couldn't talk to the coach during games. The contract also said that the coach was law and if a player talked back or was late for practice he would be benched for the game. Then they prayed to kill the other team before every game.

I wonder how the Pitcher will handle the pregame speech. He doesn't seem like a dude who likes to talk much. Everyone sits on the bench in the dugout and I know they are wondering where Mom is. The Pitcher smokes a couple cigarettes and runs the hitting drills with me catching. He runs them just like Mom with a pop-up and then a grounder and then a run into home. Everybody just goes along, but he has to say something. So we all gather around by the dugout.

The Pitcher scratches his cheek, then spits in the dust with Mom's hat on the back of his head.

"I'm Coach Jack and I'll be taking Maria's place for the game," he says, looking everyone in the eye. "I think you boys should know that your coach is in the hospital."

I stare at the ground and feel everyone staring at me.

"I think you boys know that Coach Maria loves baseball and loves you boys and would be here if there was any possible way." The Pitcher pauses again and rubs his neck. "So I think we should win this one for her."

Everybody nods.

"Now we are playing Tri City. I know a lot of you have heard they are pretty good. You have to put that out of your head." The Pitcher hocks a big glob of tobacco. "They are just like you and put their pants on one leg at a time too. So let's win this one for Coach Maria and ..." He pauses and his voice falls, just for a moment. "And ... let's all say a prayer for her."

The Pitcher tilts his head down and the team waits. I squeeze my eyes shut and ask God for the hundredth time to spare Mom. That's how I see it. I know he has to spare her and let her stay with me. I squeeze my eyes hard, trying to throw my thoughts up into space. I figure God has to be up there somewhere.

39

HEAT TAKES OVER GAMES LIKE an extra player. Kids get slow, some pass out, some lose it and they just want to sit on the bench. Today, kids are already drinking Gatorade and water and taking ice cubes and putting them inside their hats. Florida has dropped a hundred-degree day on the field and everyone is struggling against the heat rising out of the infield. The umpire looks really hot after the first inning and drinks from a big orange thermos just behind the fence. Only the Pitcher seems unaffected by the heat, smoking and spitting. He leans against the dugout like a picture of an old-time ballplayer.

The game starts and Coach Gino's strategy is out in front. Find a team's Achilles heel, you know, the one thing that will make them fall apart. He starts right away questioning calls and asking for clarifications on rules. He wants to draw in our coach and get him to lose his game. The first few innings start out with us holding Tri City to one run. Their cleanup man blasts one between second and third and brings in another run when our shortstop misses the ball. Artie pitches and Gino watches while our catcher throws down to second.

"*You're up, you're up!*" he shouts.

The Tri City runner doesn't even have to slide.

"Get off that bag. *Let's go!*" Gino shouts.

The next four innings run back and forth. Then Eric knocks three down with a breaking fastball and a curve. I take out the first batter with three straight fastballs. The second batter I bring down with a couple sinkers and finish him with a fastball. I'm in *the zone* and that's why I know Gino will start something.

"BLUE, THAT WAS A BALK."

I had just thrown a beautiful inside pitch that smacked like a starter pistol. Tri City is quiet. A pitch just under eighty miles an hour shuts up just about everybody. The balk thing is all Gino needs. I start into my windup again.

"*BALK, BLUE!*"

The Tri City crowd picks up on the balk chant. *Balk! Balk! Balk!* I had a one-and-one count and I knew the last pitch was in the zone. I bring my hands together and shift the ball in my glove. Even my mitt is burning hot from the sun.

"BALK, BLUE!"

Gino screams so loud it makes me jump.

"Balk! Take a base," the umpire shouts.

That's when the Pitcher walks on the field and Gino trots out.

"That ain't no balk," the Pitcher declares loudly.

It's kind of funny because the Pitcher is really big and Gino is this little skinny Puerto Rican guy. The umpire takes off his mask and stands between them. I see Gino shrugging like he has nothing to do with it. He spreads his arms wide.

"I saw the balk where I was standing!"

The Pitcher spits tobacco juice at Gino's feet.

"Bull!"

Now the umpire is staring at the Pitcher.

"It's not my fault your Pitcher doesn't know the rules of the game," Gino continues, laying it on.

The Pitcher spits again.

"That's what I think of your balk, rockhead."

Gino laughs. His white teeth are moving under his Oakleys. He is playing his game, man. You draw them in and then you piss them off—the coach first and then the team. You get teams so mad they don't know what they're doing. He's all into the psychological play.

"Oh and you know all about balks?" Gino continues.

"Yeah, I do, rockhead," the Pitcher replies. "They tried to change the rule on me and they couldn't do it in the series."

I know about Gino, man. I know he tried for a slot and played Single A ball for a while. I know how much he respected the game. And that's why I know Gino doesn't know who he is dealing with. He cracks this big smile and says real loud, "What series was that? *The 1902 series?*"

"Seventy-eight, rockhead."

Gino stares at him and blinks twice. I mean Gino *knows* baseball. He knows all the great games and the Series in '78 had several great games. He knows all about Mariano and Langford and their historic duel. He stares at the big dude with the bump of tobacco in his lip. Even from the mound I can see his mouth hanging open.

"Oh, right. Seventy-eight. Sure, sure." He laughs again uneasily and claps his hands. "So you're Jack Langford and I'm Bob Mariano, right?"

"You ain't no Bob Mariano," the Pitcher says.

Gino tilts his head as the umpire whips out his phone. He looks at the Pitcher, then his phone. I know he is Googling him right there. He looks up with the phone in his palm.

"I'll be damned. Are you Jack Langford?"

The Pitcher nods.

"Yeah."

"I'll be damned," the umpire cries out. "I can't believe it," he says, shaking the Pitcher's hand. "I just can't fricking believe it! Jack Langford is coaching in my game! I saw that Series! You got a home run off of Bob Mariano and then struck him out!"

Gino is staring at the Pitcher, then the umpire.

"How did you ever come to coach a league team?"

"I'm filling in for a friend."

Gino hovers around the ump like a pesky bug.

"Blue, what about the call?"

The umpire looks at Gino like he forgot all about the game. He turns back to the Pitcher and you can see he regrets the call. I think he just wanted to ask the Pitcher about the World Series, but Gino is raising a big stink now.

"The balk call stands," he says, "but let me worry about making the calls from now on."

"Oh yeah, no problem, Blue," Gino mumbles. "But he was balking."

The umpire stares at the Pitcher as he walks back to our dugout.

"Jack Langford ... unbelievable," he says, shaking his head.

40

BABE RUTH SAID HE ALWAYS swung big with everything he had. He said he wanted to win big or lose big. I like that, you know. I'm not the greatest batter and figure I might as well go for it.

Here's what happens: We come alive and tie up the game. The Pitcher moves our players around with Toby Yostremski at short. Toby makes quick work of a grounder with a double play. A throw down from the catcher to second ends the inning. I hold Tri City to a single hit!

The Tri City crowd grows quiet as we come up to bat again. They figure they will blow us out. Scores like twenty-two to nothing happen. But baseball is all about momentum. You lose the momentum and you lose the game.

So the Tri City side gets real quiet. They have been yelling stuff like:

"SIT DOWN. HE CAN'T PITCH. GO HOME."

"HE CANT HIT THE ZONE."

"HE'S DONE."

Now we are the ones making a racket.

All we have to do is get our bats going.

Eric has been knocking them down and takes the mound at the top of the seventh. He takes out our first two batters with his cutter. He has a medium fastball, but his cutter really moves and pinches the outside corner. Our batters foul off twice and then he throws an inside fastball when they try to adjust. It works beautifully. Devin always told him to know what he was going to do before you get to the mound. He does.

Then it is my bat. The Pitcher and I never worked on my batting, but he said it required the same type of concentration. *"You pick a spot. You have to see yourself hitting the ball. When I belted that homerun in the Series, I saw it before I swung. I had picked a spot over the centerfield fence and that's where I hit it."* It was hard for me to believe anyone could pick a spot in a World Series and then hit the ball to that spot. But the Pitcher swore that's what happened. And he did it.

"Two cutters, then an inside fastball is what he has," he tells me outside the dugout, looking at Eric. "Just crowd the plate for that inside fastball and you'll force him off his game."

I walk up to home plate with my heart thumping and my hands sweaty. I tap the rubber with my bat, then snatch up some dirt and rub it into my gloves. Eric grins on the mound.

"C'mon, Eric ... take it home!"

"One more, Eric!"

"You got this guy ... one, two, three!"

I step out of the box and take a couple swings and feel my shoulders tighten. I roll my arms to try and loosen up. I take one more swing, then snug my gloves and go into the box. I stretch out the bat and extend toward the mound, then hunch down and bring it to my shoulder. Blue guns his finger and I watch Eric set himself. I move the bat in a tight circle, tensing my shoulders, locking on his hands. He looks over his mitt and stares at me.

I hear the catcher adjust his stance, shifting his mitt. I hear the umpire grunt as he bends down and the parents scream. *"C'mon, Eric, bring us home! One, two, three, Eric! You got this, guy!"* Eric breaks his hands and kicks high, then I hear that sonic whistle as the ball rockets past me.

"Streeeerike!"

I lose the ball. I blink and lose sight of it. I step out of the box and swing again, trying to loosen up my shoulders. Eric takes the ball back and spits toward me. I swing again. No more of that. His cutter will be his demise. The Tri City crowd screams.

"Way to go, Eric!"

"That's one!"

"Two more, Eric!"

"You got him!"

I swing twice outside the box as the Pitcher motions me forward. *Crowd the plate. Crowd the plate. He will give you two cutters and then come inside with his fastball.* I pick up some more dirt from the ground and rub the bat with my gloves. I can smell the dirt on the bat like a wet field. I wonder what Mom is doing right now. Is she still breathing? Is she thinking about me? I see her in the hospital bed under the white sheets. She has all the tubes and wires and her eyes have the dark circles. Mom opens her eyes and speaks:

Keep your eye on the ball. Don't swing at any flies, Ricky. Make him give you a good one. You can do this!

I step into the box and hoist the bat and stare at the center-field fence. There is a church steeple in the distance. That is my spot. Eric stares over his mitt and grins. I keep my bat moving, keep my legs bent, weight centered. My heart booms slowly. I move the bat on my shoulder as Eric kicks back and brings the heat. His pitch breaks down to the outside.

"Steeeerike!"

Eric takes the ball again and shakes his head. I pound the plate and reset myself. I know with two strikes he could play

games. I fully expect some off-speed garbage. The problem is I
see myself getting the third strike. It's hard to come back from
a zero-and-two count. You feel like he already has you. I hear
Mom again. She's talking to me from the hospital bed in her
pajamas with the small blue flowers.

*Ignore him, Ricky. Play your game. You can do it, Ricky.
Just concentrate.*

I step out again from the box and make Eric break his set. I
take three swings and hear the bat fan the air.

"HE'S FINISHED!"

"ONE MORE, ERIC!"

"HE CAN'T HIT!"

The Tri City team is on the fence and shaking it like crazy.
I swing a couple more times and look at the Pitcher. *Make him
play your game.* That's what his slouch said to me. I step back
into the box and lean across the plate. I remember the Pitcher
once told me Bob Mariano tried to sucker him in the Series. He
threw a couple by his chin to piss him off. He said he knew
Mariano would give him one decent pitch. The Pitcher waited
until he got the pitch and slammed the home run out of the
stadium.

I keep that in mind as Eric throws three fast outside curves.
I almost take the bait on the last one.

"Full count!"

I dig in close and lean over the plate. Eric stares at me. His
catcher is giving him all sorts of signals, but he keeps shaking
them off. I'm too far over the plate. If he tries the inside fastball,
it will hit me. Eric looks over his glove, his eyes like two pieces of
cobalt. I set myself and pick out the church steeple again.

Eric kicks into his windup and his arm whips over the top.
The baseball blasts toward me like a white rocket. I swing from
my shoulder, feeling the contact through my hands.

PING!

The bat rings like the perfect note of a symphony.

PING!

I know the sound. I have heard it before when other guys hit home runs.

PING!

You know when you hit the sweet spot of the bat.

PING! PING! PING!

You can hear it in the stands.

I watch the ball shoot for the moon and clear the back fence, heading for that church steeple. I run the bases like the Babe with small steps, taking my time. I see Eric with his mouth open, staring at the back fence. He turns around and watches me jog past third. I have just hit a home run in the high school stadium.

I tap home plate and meet my teammates flooding out of the dugout.

Just like the movies, man.

Then Gino strikes again.

41

YEAH, I LOOKED UP AT the coaches' booth when I slammed
that home run over the fence. I saw Coach Poppers stand and
I felt like waving. I wanted to wave and make sure he wouldn't
forget me: the Mexican kid who just shot the ball over the fence.
But I didn't wave. I jogged those bases thinking Mom would have
loved to see this. She just got so high, man, whenever I finally
did well at something. It's like all her hope would get bottled up
and finally it could all just come out at once.

But then again, I should have known Gino wouldn't just
roll over. I don't think Google has been such a great thing for
baseball. I mean without Google you would have to carry around
the rules and most coaches don't do that. And if they do carry
them then they don't read through to find the rule they can use
against the other team. But search engines have changed all of
that. All Gino had to do was punch in rules for batters in the
KCBL. And the result:

Batters are not allowed to wear jewelry of any kind. Any violation is an automatic out.

So he waited until Eric threw that fastball down the middle. He waited until I tap danced the plate and my teammates flooded out and slapped me on the back and cheered. He waited until the high school coaches sat down in their booth. Then he rushed out pointing to my neck with his iPhone in one hand.

"Jewelry, Blue! Jewelry, Blue! Automatic out!"

I have this coral necklace Mom bought me when she went to Shell City. I usually wear it inside my jersey, but it had slipped up on my neck. The umpire stared at me and the Pitcher was out of the dugout. Gino screamed like a hyena.

"Jewelry, jewelry! No necklaces or bracelets. Automatic out!"

Now, the ump has his face mask off and is squinting at my necklace. Gino holds up his phone. *Jewelry?* I stand outside the dugout and all the parents are on their feet. This could be the game right here. I hope the umpire will tell Gino to get the hell back to his dugout. The ump slowly turns around. He looks at me, then his eyes go to the necklace around my neck. He hooks his thumb and shouts, *"Out!"*

The place goes crazy. People are booing. People are throwing things onto the field. Parents are screaming and Eric is grinning. It is dirty baseball, but there is nothing we can do. I turn and see Mrs. Payne by the fence. She is staring at me like she had planned it all. Mom said she had thrown a fit when she heard I had an MLB coach. She even called the league commissioner to see if it was legal.

I watch the Pitcher shake his head.

"Jewelry! Jewelry! Come on, Blue!"

The ump holds his hands out.

"That's the league rule ... no jewelry. Automatic out!"

Gino is grinning like crazy, man. It is pure Gino and I can see he got his mojo back after the whole balk thing. He's the man with the rules and he just pulled off probably his greatest play.

Nobody ever enforced the jewelry rule, but nobody played like Gino either.

"That's pure bullshit, Blue," the Pitcher shouts.

The ump crosses his arms.

"That's my ruling and I'd like you to go back to your dugout," he says, like he's only going to say it once.

I can tell he's not playing around. The Pitcher kicks dirt on him. He kicks it just like Lou Piniella, getting in his face.

"You're letting this asshole play dirty ball," he yells. "This guy is a joke, Blue, and you're playing his game!"

"That's it," the umpire shouts, jabbing his finger toward the stands. "Go back to your dugout or I'm throwing you out!"

"C'mon," I say, grabbing the Pitcher's arm.

"He can't throw me out," he shouts.

"Don't be a rockhead. Of course he can," I tell him.

The Pitcher stares at me.

"Yeah. You're right," he mutters, walking back to the dugout.

Blue is still staring at him and I remember articles about Jack Langford's temper and how he would argue and get thrown out of games. I don't want him to get thrown out because we still need him. *I need him.* I know how Gino rolls and he wants nothing more than for our coach to get ejected. I have seen it happen before with other teams. I mean, I know the Pitcher played in the MLB, man, for twenty-five years and won the World Series and was the MVP.

But he's never faced people who want their kid to make the high school team.

42

YOU KNOW WHAT MY BIGGEST fear is? That I really don't have talent and I have been fooling myself and Mom and the Pitcher all along. Maybe making the high school freshman team is impossible. My arm is not special. I am not special. I am just like every other kid with big dreams. It happens, you know. People believe something their whole life that has nothing to do with reality. It's like a big bluff. Maybe that's me, because I'm blowing it again. And the worst thing is ...

Eric has just come up to bat.

In the next life, man, I want blue eyes because you get a lot of things, you know. You get to be the Pitcher. I knew when they pulled back my home run there was no way a Mexican kid was going to push off a white dude. Same way with Mom. She knew when she passed that petition around at Target she was done and would lose her job. Now I understand why she did it. She must have done it for pride, you know.

For respect.

So I'm pitching for pride now. I'm pitching for Mom. It's the bottom of the seventh. Even after they called back my home run, we manage to get up by one. Eric walks Jerry and Jerry is this Japanese dude who can really hit the ball. He's good at short too because he's so compact and low to the ground. The thing with small kids is it's really hard to hit the zone. In fact it's almost impossible for me, and Eric has the same problem. Then Ronnie steals third and Toby shoots one down the third baseline bringing Ronnie in.

Eric mows down our next batter.

So now I'm going out to pitch and, yeah, you guessed it, things are not going well. My head is like up in space somewhere around Jupiter. I take down the first two batters with a couple fastballs and a sinker. Then I start seeing Mom in those white hospital sheets and all those tubes and wires that are draining her life. I can't stop thinking she's dying.

My next pitch flies over Ronnie's head and rings the backstop. The next pitch trenches the dirt and bounces up into Blue's mask. Then I pinch the corners and Blue calls everyone. The first batter walks. The second batter clips one down the third baseline for a single. I ring the backstop on two fastballs and a breaking ball that puffs the dirt. My last pitch cuts the batter's knees and he walks.

And now bases are loaded. The Pitcher stands there with his arms crossed by the dugout. To me he looks like he's part of the dugout, part of the field. He belongs there. It's me that's the odd piece. And then Eric walks up to bat swinging his Titanium Slugger like he is Hercules. He swings outside the box, smacks the plate three times, then lines the bat up like he's aiming a gun.

I'm staring him down and he's giving it back to me with those weird blue eyes. The bat spins and hovers on his shoulder while the umpire hunches down. All I can think is Eric never strikes out. He *destroys* the ball. He creams the ball and sends it over the back fence like some kind of machine. He has logged hundreds, maybe *thousands* of hours in batting cages. He has a stout body and big shoulders that got bigger from weight lifting. He can smash the ball into orbit if he wants to.

And I have loaded the bases.

If I walk him I will tie it up. If I give him anything in the zone, I'll lose the game. The worst thing is he knows my fastball. He has seen it a million times. Forget that I'm not even hitting the zone. If I do hit the zone then he will belt it for the stars, man. And all I can think about is Mom. I just want to go to the hospital and make sure she's alright. I really hope the Pitcher will pull me and let somebody else blow the game.

But he doesn't. He just stands there chewing, spitting, watching. I bring my hands together and try to clear my mind. Eric's bat revolves like a serpent ready to strike. I take a breath and kick back and go for an inside fastball, but my release is too early and the ball nearly flies over Ronnie's head. Eric stands up and grins.

I take the ball from Ronnie and look down. *Take your time, Ricky. Take your time. I want you to breathe. You can do this.* I set myself, breathing in the rawhide of my mitt. I close my eyes, take another breath, and throw a fastball down the line. Eric blasts it toward first base and the ball goes foul. He pounds the plate, then sets himself again. I throw a sinker down the middle. He chips it for the fence down the third baseline. Foul. One-two count. Eric's nodding to me, grinning. *Bring it on* is what he says. I bring everything I have and throw wild and ring the backstop like the bell of a fight ending. And I figure the fight has ended, because it is the best I've had.

And all I can think about now is seeing Mom.

Two-two count.

Now I know what is going on. All the bad things are coming together. And I know I Mom is running out of time. I'm running out of time.

Then the Pitcher calls a time-out.

***

"You're going to have to give this guy something else. He knows your fastball and the next one ain't going to go foul."

The Pitcher says that while he's looking at Eric, smoking the dust with tobacco juice. He turns around and pushes back Mom's cap.

"You got any idea what you want to do with this guy?"

I look down at the ball and shake my head.

"Well, you gotta do something."

I look up into the Pitcher's grey eyes.

"Mom is really sick ... isn't she?"

I ask him in a way where he can't lie. The Pitcher doesn't move even when the breeze lifts his hat. We both stand there in the dust whipping up from the infield. His lips protrude, his eyes becoming winter.

"Yeah," he says, and he has to look away. I know then.

Mom is dying.

He looks back at me.

"But she wants you to finish the game, Ricky. That's her wish."

They come just like that. The tears sit on the oiled leather of my glove—the oil Mom had put on when she put my glove in the oven and baked it. We had a good laugh over that. The house smelled like warm leather. Now I'm thinking about the time Mom found me with my head against the refrigerator. I couldn't stop crying because I couldn't remember the signals in a game. Mom rubbed my shoulders and we went over the signals for hours.

And I remembered every signal the next game.

But now I can't stop wondering, *Who will rub my shoulders now? Who will teach me the signals, you know? Who will sit on the porch with me and go over my homework or make pancakes on Saturday morning?*

I hold the glove over my eyes and breathe heavily.

"I can't do it. I can't pitch."

I hear the Pitcher spit again.

"Look at me, son."

I look up and his eyes have changed. They are softer ... softer than I have ever seen.

"It's your mom's dream ... for you to play on the high school team. It's her wish for you to have your dream. So you and I gotta make sure that happens." He pauses again, his eyes blood red, his face leathered from time. "You got more guts than any kid I ever knew. More goddamn guts than I ever did, and I want you to know something: Your Mom loves you and always will."

And then, his eyes get kind of wet. Like water on old parchment or something. He wipes his eyes and pulls this dusty paper out of his pocket.

"Look, your mom told me to give it to you if you got in trouble," he mutters, handing me the paper. "I figure you need it now."

I open the paper slowly and there's Mom's perfect handwriting with the little swirls and curlicues. I have seen these notes a thousand times. She put one in my lunch every day telling me to always believe in myself. I smell the paper and catch her perfume. Then I begin to read.

Ricky,

I know you are having trouble. Just remember that you can do anything you want if you put your mind to it. Don't worry about me. I will always be there for you. I will always be with you. Just take your breath and listen to what Mr. Langford tells you. Remember I will always love you and that will never change. You are becoming a fine young man and a great baseball player. I couldn't be prouder of you. Now take your breath, find your quiet space,

and use the gift God gave you.
    I love you.

    Love you forever,

    Mom

    P.S. Take your breath!

The tears rush my eyes again because Mom is telling me: *Just do it again, Ricky. You can do this.* And I just keep swinging and swinging and she is buying me a mitt and a ball and a bat and we are selling candy at the Jewel for the team and she's there every time in the dugout when I come off the field. We are working on my homework again and she's sending me to school with my backpack and telling me to have a great day.

And then I just see it. I know why I have to finish.

Mom has always been there for me and I have to be here for her now.

"We're out of time, bud," the Pitcher says.

I look up and see the umpire waiting and Eric glaring with the bat on his shoulder. I see Mrs. Payne behind the backstop staring at me. I put the note inside my jersey and nod.

"Yeah ... I'm ready."

He puts his hand on my shoulder.

"Remember what you did that first day? Remember you asked me to pitch your way? Well do it now. Pitch *your way.* What I have taught you is part of you now. Don't worry about it. Reach down inside yourself and pitch the way you know how."

He pauses.

"Use your gift."

I look down and breathe deeply.

"OK," I say. "Let's play ball."

43

YOU HAVE TO WONDER WHAT the Pitcher is thinking in that final game of the Series. The series is tied and they are in game seven with Detroit up by one. It's a full count and the Cardinals have a man on third. Two outs. The game is in the Pitcher's hands and he knows it. He knows in that smoke-filled stadium he's on top of the mountain. He has to deliver the pitch that will make him a hero or a bum for the rest of his life. As he said that first day, the whole world is a full count against you.

And then he winds up and comes in with a sinker. The batter swings and the ball pops straight up and his catcher flings his mask as I reach out and grab the ball thirty-three years later. You can't blame me for grabbing it. Everybody wants to grab the ball at some time in their life, right? Like the Fan.

You just go for it.

I'm standing in the middle of Wildcat Stadium, gripping the ball and looking down the batter just like the Pitcher. And I know this will define me. Nothing that comes before or after will matter more than this moment. I'm staring at Eric and thinking about Jack Langford's first pitch. He called it his *get-the-hell-back pitch*. He always threw a ninety-mile-an-hour fastball by the batter's chin. He said it let the batter know who was boss and gave him room to pinch the corners.

When he went against Bob Mariano he gave him two curves and figured Mariano would expect a fastball on a two-and-one count. So he threw another curve and got him to swing for a two-two count. He then threw another curve and let it go to a full count. He then went with the slider. *"Break it down at the last minute while he tastes the home run."* That's how he put it. *"So I threw it in there under him. He had to swing ... that's how mad he was about that home run I got off of him. That's how much I got in his head."*

And now Eric is moving his bat like he's going to kill the ball. The Tri City and Marauder teams are in the front of their dugouts. Parents shout from both sides. A slight haze rolls under the lights in the early darkness.

Eric and I stare down the seventy feet separating us. I find my spot. I find it in his toothy grin and his eyes that taunt me like blue lasers. I hear his mother yell.

"HE'S NOTHING, ERIC. YOU GOT HIM!"

I hear Eric:

"Don't hit me, beano. I will kick your ass if you do!"

I breathe in my glove and see something flicker through his eyes. I close my eyes, then deliver my get-the-hell-back pitch. Eric dives for the ground. And then he jumps up and charges the mound. Just like I knew he would. I duck his first swing and Gino has him before he takes a second. He shouts as the umpire comes between us.

"YOU DID IT ON PURPOSE! YOU DID IT ON PURPOSE!"

I brush myself off while Gino walks him back. Eric shakes off Gino and swears as he grabs his bat from the ground. He swings outside the batter's box like a wild man, then points the bat at me and mouths, *You're dead, beano.*

I look over at the Pitcher. He just nods.

Full count.

I can't hear myself think, because everyone is going crazy. Eric is glaring as I take the ball from Ronnie. He's swinging his bat like an executioner and daring me to put anything in the zone. His face is red. He steps in with his bat moving like an angry creature. I set myself and breathe deeply and close my eyes. I can hear the crowd, feel the breeze, smell the infield dirt. I know who this pitch is for, first and last. I see Mom in her bed, breathing lightly, waiting for me to finish.

Go ahead. It's your moment to shine, Ricky.

I position the ball in the back of my hand, then bring my hands to my set. I adjust my grip and tuck in my arm.

Breathe, Ricky.

I breathe again. There is only silence. Eric is gritting his teeth, moving his bat. The wind blows sand around us. The umpire is waiting. I stand on the mound completely alone. I close my eyes and kick up my leg, then explode forward and lasso my arm down and scrape the blackboard with my fingers.

Eric sees what he wants to see. He sees that fastball coming in straight and level and *expects* it to get to him. He expects the only pitch I ever had and gets out in front of it. He swings hard, he swings mad, he swings at that fifty-mile-an-hour pitch like it's going seventy-five. And I watch his shoulders bring the bat around as the umpire jams his fist out to the side.

"Steeeerike!

And then Eric just stares at me. He stares at me in that terrific silence that is baseball. He stares like I just cheated him out of his life. Then like someone turning up a stereo all the way, the stadium goes crazy. We just beat Tri City. We just beat the championship team. And now I'm running and I know where I'm going. I knew it when I saw that picture in the Pitcher's garage, because Ronnie, our catcher, has thrown his mask and is running toward me.

We meet halfway out from the plate and I jump up and he catches me. We both scream to the heavens. And someone snaps a picture.

44

HOSPITALS CREEP ME OUT, LIKE I said. This one is new and looks like some kind of space station with a helicopter port and this circular dome that patients walk around in. The Pitcher pulls up near the emergency room and we walk in quickly. I feel like Mom might die any minute. Now I'm walking down a white hallway clutching the game ball with my cleats clicking on the floor. People stare at the Mexican kid in the dirty baseball uniform and the big guy with the too small hat, the craggy face, faded sweats, and ancient cleats.

We walk right past the nurse's station into Mom's room and a different world. She is under all these tubes and wires and monitors with the jumping green spike. I stand in my cleats and uniform, not able to move. We are too late. She is as white as her sheets and not moving as the electronics beep and hum and whir. I breathe in the rubbing alcohol Mom uses when I get splinters. I start to cry when she opens her eyes.

"Ricky," she murmurs.

I come by her bed and Mom holds up her hands. I hug her thin body with the tubes going over her shoulders. I don't want to hug too hard because she feels like a doll that might break. I can smell the faint lemony perfume that's her. Her skin has faded to a light brown as if someone had pulled away the color. I can't keep my eyes from fuzzing up, but I try. Ain't no time to fall apart, you know.

"We won, Mom!" I say, holding up the game ball. "I brought you the ball. All the guys signed it. I got a home run and then I pitched and threw a change-up and won the game for us!"

I'm rushing. I'm rushing because I feel like she might leave. I have been rushing ever since the Pitcher drove like a maniac through Jacksonville. Mom holds the grass-stained ball, inky from all the signatures. A slight glow rises to her cheeks and I stare down at the white sheets, because I'm having trouble keeping it together.

"A change-up," she says softly. "I always knew that's all you needed."

"Yeah, it worked beautifully," I say, wiping my eyes quickly.

Mom smiles with tears on her eyelashes.

"You did it, Ricky," she murmurs again, looking at me. "You will be on the high school team now. Those high school coaches saw you play and win the game."

"Yeah," I say, nodding, but I feel no joy.

All I want now is for Mom to leave and we will go to McDonald's and talk about the game. Then we will go home and she will tell me to get my bat bag out of the car and yell about wearing cleats in the house. Then we will buy a new mitt or go online and look at bats. Maybe we will go to the batting cages or talk about the high school team and the coaches and the players and laugh around the kitchen table. I just want her to leave this person sitting under all these tubes and wires.

Mom smiles again, a faint fire in her eyes.

"I told you, Ricky ... you could be whoever you wanted and

do whatever you want." She closes her eyes. "And you did it ... you learned how to pitch and became ... the pitcher."

I lean down and put my head on her pillow. I can't help it.

Mom pats my head like she has a thousand times before.

"I love you, Ricky," she whispers.

***

I go downstairs to get something to drink and when I come back, Grandma is there. The Pitcher is next to the bed and holds Mom's hand. He's really big in the room. He has his hat off and his hair is puffed up. He looks caged to me. His big hands cover Mom's and his weathered cheeks are like a rough sculpture against the smooth white room.

Mom wakes up and he leans close.

"How are you, tough lady?" he asks gently.

"Not so tough anymore," she murmurs, keeping her eyes half-closed.

I look at the flowers by her bed. Mom speaks in Spanish and Grandma nods.

"Hi, Grandma," I say.

Mom lets the Pitcher's hand go and I can tell even that tires her out. She had waited too long. That's what the doctor said. *She had waited too long.* And again I asked, *too long for what?* I knew, but I didn't want to know, if that makes any sense. My feeling was that if she could get away from these tubes and from this hospital, then she would be fine. I knew it wasn't true, but that's what I thought.

"You did it, Maria," the Pitcher tells her. "Everyone saw Ricky pitch and win the game. The coaches were in the booth. The freshman coach congratulated him personally," he continues like an announcer.

Mom wipes her eyes and smiles again. I know the Pitcher's play is to let Mom know everything is going to be fine. I am down with that. Let her know her work is over. We are a team on this. The Pitcher said in the parking lot the best thing we could do is let Mom know everything is fine. That way she can concentrate on getting well.

"It was a beautiful change-up," the Pitcher continues, shaking his head. "He struck out that Eric kid like a pro."

"I figured Eric would never expect that," I add quickly, nodding.

Mom stares at the Pitcher and frowns.

"You taught him a change-up? I thought you didn't believe in them."

"I don't," he replies, rolling his shoulders. "But for some people ... a change-up is right."

Mom tries to sit up and then she grimaces.

"Are you alright, Mom?"

"I'm fine," she answers faintly as Dr. Aziz comes back in.

Her doctor says she has to do an examination. She sees the game ball and glares as if that was the reason Mom got sick. You could blame it on baseball. I wanted to, but then you wouldn't understand Mom. Baseball and Mom have become all mixed up somewhere.

She holds her hand out again to the Pitcher. Her eyes glass up.

"Thank you," she whispers. "Thank you."

I watch the Pitcher try to speak, amazed as his lower lip trembles. He keeps his eyes down and doesn't move. I have never seen such a big man cry before. I mean, you just don't think really big dudes ever cry. But they do, man. They do.

45

I STAY IN THE GARAGE with the Pitcher that night. Grandma stays at the hospital. He flips on a game—Cardinals and Mets. He gives me a Coke and cracks a beer and pulls up another armchair. Shortstop sleeps on his back with the night crickets outside and it seems like the world of hospitals is a million miles away. I slump down in my uniform while the Pitcher smokes cigarettes and drinks his beer.

"Hey."

"Yeah."

I turn to him and squint.

"How come you never had kids?"

The Pitcher taps his cigarette in a beer can.

"Maybe I was too wrapped up with my career." He tilts his head, the television flickering over his face. "Betty wanted them, but I told her I was too much of a kid. She would have been a great mother."

I stare at the game for a moment.

"What was she like?"

"Great," he pauses. "She was great."

"She sounds great."

He put his cigarette in his beer.

"I was a rockhead. We should have had kids. I shouldn't have always put baseball over everything."

"Maybe that's what she loved about you," I say sleepily.

"Yeah, maybe."

"Is that why you drink?"

"I drink because of a lot of things." He leans back and shuts his eyes halfway. "I moved into this lousy garage because every time I turned around she was there. This was the only place where things were still good."

I stare at the old pictures on the wall.

"Like when you pitched?"

"Yeah," he says. "Like when I pitched."

46

DR. AZIZ SAID THE NEXT week would be critical. The Pitcher stays in his garage and helps out where he can. None of us knows what to do, because all we can do is wait. We see Mom and then we realize this uses up her strength. Joey and I go back to throwing in the street and messing around. It is hot and I can't concentrate on anything. Throwing a ball just isn't the same. The Pitcher sits in his garage and watches television.

A lot of times I sit with him and we watch baseball. Four days after our big game he is making dinner for us. His dinners are the same: burgers, hotdogs, burgers, Italian beef, burgers, steak. We have meat and meat and meat.

The phone rings and he picks up.

"Hello," he says, and then after a pause adds, "No, I'm a personal family friend."

I look up from the Cubs versus the Sox. The Pitcher holds the phone to his ear and has this strange look on his face. I feel my heart and freeze right there on the couch. I have seen this moment a hundred times already. Grandma looks up from her knitting and turns white. The Pitcher has the worst expression I have ever seen on anybody.

He hangs up and stares at the phone. Finally he walks into the living room and looks at me.

"I don't see how they can do that," he says slowly.

I stare at him, feeling my eyes fill with hot tears. She's gone. The world has just left down a long dark tunnel and I want to go after Mom. I can't stay in the world with her gone. The Pitcher shakes his head slowly

"What!" I cry out, staggering up from the couch. "Just say it, man!"

He frowns.

"How did you know?"

"I can tell," I wailed with the tears blinding me.

It's what I suspected all along. She had gone under from all those tubes and wires in that funky space station hospital. How could anyone live in a place like that? It's where people go to die.

"How did it happen," I sniffle, wiping my eyes

The Pitcher shakes his head.

"I'm not sure. I just don't see how they can keep you from trying out."

I stop crying and stare at him.

"You mean ... you mean that wasn't the hospital?"

The Pitcher lights a cigarette.

"Nah. That was the coach for the high school team."

"You mean ..." I breathe again. "You mean Mom is alright then?"

He raises his eyebrows, staring at me like I have lost my mind.

"Last I heard." He shrugs. "I talked to her about an hour ago. She wasn't doing great, but she's hanging in there."

Hanging in there. What beautiful words, man. Grandma claps and I dance like a fool. *Mom is still alive.* I sit on the couch and stare at the Pitcher. I feel myself come back to earth and then things get real heavy.

"What do you mean ... *I can't try out?*"

The Pitcher breathes smoke into the living room.

"This Payne woman, that kid's mother, sent the commissioner something saying your mother is an illegal alien and you shouldn't be in the school," he says, looking at me. "So they ain't going to let you try out."

I stare at him, feeling my stomach hollow. *Wetback.* That's what the Pitcher just said to me. I saw Mrs. Payne's glare and it said one thing to me, man: She *hates* us. She hates us for who we are and will do anything to make sure her son comes first. It all started to make sense—Grandma coming to live with us and why Mom had stared at that link Mrs. Payne had sent us.

The Pitcher looks at me and frowns.

"Is your mother here illegally?"

I feel my face get hot. I think about how she lived in Arizona and then went to Chicago. Joey said a lot of Mexicans came in through Texas and a lot through Arizona. He said his uncle snuck across the border and got a phony Social Security card and started working like twenty years ago.

"I don't know," I say, looking at him.

The Pitcher smokes for a moment, his eyes dark.

"Your mother is more of a goddamn American than anybody I know and this is complete bullshit."

He flicks his ash into his palm.

"Eric will be the pitcher after all," I mutter.

"Don't be a goddamn rockhead."

I stare at him. "If I can't try out, then how am I going to pitch?"

The Pitcher continues staring into space. A horrible thought occurs to me that makes me sick to my stomach. It is so bad I can't even really think about it. But if I can't even try out for the team, then everything Mom has worked for will have been in vain. She is in that hospital bed for nothing. I can't think about that. The thought that the *Mrs. Paynes* of the world would win is just too much.

"One thing is for sure," he says, looking at me. "Your mother is not to know about this until I can fix it somehow."

He sat for a moment.

"It would kill her."

47

I SIT ON THE PORCH that evening and watch Shortstop
walk by the slot a few times. Then I see the Pitcher pacing back
and forth. He usually just settles in with his Good Times and his
Skoal and cigarettes and watches game after game, but tonight
he walks from one side of his garage to the other. He sits at the
kitchen table a long time after the phone call. Then he turns on
the news and watches the Mexicans demonstrating in Arizona.

He keeps staring, ashing his cigarette.

As I watch him, I think about his last years. He had stayed
with Detroit for another seven years after the Series, but then
he started to lose. In 1985 he lost eighteen games. It happens
to pitchers. They start to slow and their delivery starts to fade.
For some guys it is very sudden. They lose their fastball or they
blow out their shoulder. But for the Pitcher it was a long, slow
descent where he couldn't get the outs anymore. Detroit traded
him away to the Mets where he stayed for a year and only won
eight games and lost thirteen. Then he retired for a couple years

and ran a restaurant before coming back as a free agent.

He signed with the Padres for a year, then retired for good in 1995.

He never pitched again.

***

I usually sack in as long as I can. So I'm not quite sure why I wake so early, then I know and feel really bad. The high school baseball tryouts begin today. I grab a bowl of cereal and go onto the porch and squint against the sun. The Pitcher is in his driveway with his garage up. He's standing there smoking and staring at his television, his couch, his kitchen with the two boards across the slop sink, and the pictures on the walls. I leave the porch and walk across the street in my T-shirt and shorts. My flip flops clap loudly as I walk up his drive . He has a cigarette in his mouth, wearing some old blue shorts, his loafers, and a faded orange golf shirt.

The Pitcher turns, his eyes bleeding red and his jaw peppered white.

"A man living in a garage," he says. "Pathetic, huh?"

I stare at the garage that had so much mystery before. Like when Joey and I used to throw stuff under the door. A man who pitched in a World Series lived there. And it did have magic, you know. In a way, I wished I could go back to thinking the Pitcher was in there. It was a little like believing in Santa Claus. It's like you know, but you don't want to know. But now, in the morning light, it looks like just a crappy old garage.

"I still think it's kind of cool."

The Pitcher shakes his head.

"No. Only a rockhead would live like this."

I don't know what to say. Adults just seem to get stuck in situations they can't get out of. Like Fernando leaving us and then coming back to steal money or the Pitcher ending up in his garage. Or Mom stuck with a deadbeat ex-husband and no job. I don't know, maybe everybody gets stuck eventually.

The Pitcher stares at the garage.

"The hardest thing about pitching ... is when it's over."

He pauses.

"Then whaddaya do?"

I blink at him and look past to his La-Z-Boy and his television. Shortstop is sitting patiently, staring at the garage as if waiting for a signal.

I roll my shoulders and look at him.

"... a change-up ... right?"

The Pitcher doesn't move, then turns slowly and stares at me. He drops his cigarette and starts walking.

"C'mon," he calls back, heading toward his car.

"Where are we going?"

"To those high school tryouts."

I frown and don't move.

"I thought they said I couldn't tryout!"

The Pitcher turns around.

"Your mother didn't go through all this shit for nothing."

48

A SPITBALL IS ILLEGAL. IT'S amazing that a little bit of spit can throw a baseball off enough where a batter can't hit it. The way a spitball works is the spit causes dirt to adhere to the ball and then it's off balance and does really weird things. Like suddenly ducking the bat or gyrating into a corner. The ball just doesn't act the way you think it will. And so they outlawed it, but a lot of guys still put grease on the ball from their glove. Anything to make a baseball do the unexpected.

The reason I bring this up is I'm not sure what's happening to the Pitcher. Something between Mom getting sick and me not trying out has produced that extra little bit of spit. Something has knocked him off balance and he is doing things nobody could predict. We don't go straight to the high school. We make a detour to the hospital first.

I ask the Pitcher if something has happened. I ask him again after we meet the dude in the parking lot with the collar. He doesn't seem like a minister or a priest though. For one thing, he has long hair and a beard and wears tennis shoes and jeans.

"Are you ... are you a priest?" I ask him from the backseat.

He smiles easily and laughs.

"Minister. You can call me Mike," he answers, shaking my hand.

"He's a coach," the Pitcher adds.

Mike nods and laughs again.

"I'm a coach too," he says. "I coach over at Trenton High School. Jack has been kind enough over the years to do some charity work for us, although I haven't heard from him for the last few years ... so this is a surprise," he finishes, looking at the Pitcher.

"Don't worry. Everything is fine," he mutters. "He's here just in case."

"Just in case of what?" I ask, very alarmed.

The Pitcher squints.

"I throw a change-up."

Then we are in the hospital and it is a lot brighter during the day and it doesn't seem like everyone there is going to die. Something about hospitals at night just creeps me out. We walk down the hallway quickly and I don't even know if it is visiting hours. The Pitcher just bulls into Mom's room and she looks up from her breakfast.

There is color in Mom's face and it seems like she has less tubes. Her hair is pulled back and I see some makeup. Mom looks at the young minister, then at the Pitcher, then me, and then her face turns straight white.

"What the hell is going on here?"

"Hello, Ms. Hernandez," Rev. Mike says, clasping her hand.

I mean Mom looks *freaked*. Wouldn't you if a minister walked in your hospital room? Mom is staring at Rev. Mike like *what the hell?* The Pitcher is standing back and then Rev. Mike puts his hand on my arm like something is about to happen.

"What is going on?" Mom demands, turning to the Pitcher.

He walks forward just like he's going to the mound and Rev. Mike squeezes my arm. Mom stares at the Pitcher like he might throw up on her. I mean, here is this big guy in his goofy shorts and his old loafers and looks like he hasn't slept all night.

Mom presses back against the bed.

"What are you—?"

And then the Pitcher goes down on his knee by her bed. I got to tell you, man, this shocks the hell out of me. This pretty Hispanic nurse steps back and everyone is staring. The room gets weirdly quiet as Mom shakes her head. But you don't tell a Pitcher anything when he's on the mound, man.

"Don't you—"

"Maria," the Pitcher says in a clear voice.

Mom is shaking her head like crazy. She leans forward and motions to him, whispering intensely. He has both his hands up on her bed like he's praying.

"Get off your knees!"

The Pitcher reaches out and takes her hand, the one with only two tubes in it. This big, worn leathery guy is holding this Mexican mother's hand in a hospital bed. The Pitcher speaks in a low voice I have never heard before. I can feel my heart bumping away so *I know* Mom must be nervous.

The Pitcher faces her and says:

"I love you, Maria Hernandez ... and I love your son, Ricky."

Mom's eyes fill and the nurse starts crying. Rev. Mike is smiling. The Pitcher brings up his other hand and leans forward. It's like I can't believe what I'm seeing. He tilts his head back and speaks in this calm voice.

"Will you marry me, Maria Hernandez? Will you marry me and make me the happiest man in the world?"

It's all so corny, but pretty cool too. I have seen this a hundred times in movies, but the real thing is a lot different. Mom is staring at the Pitcher with tears rolling down her face. She leans forward and shakes her head, asking him just above a whisper, "Why are you asking me this?"

"Because, I love you, Maria," he answers, and I know then why he was a great Pitcher—he doesn't choke. "Because you put your son's dream in front of yourself. Because you have the soul of an angel. Because I could only hope to be half as good a man as you are a woman."

And the nurse just starts bawling! Which I guess *is* like a movie and even Mike the reverend dude has tears in his eyes. Nobody speaks, because everyone is crying now, except the Pitcher. And in a way I'm shocked, but actions speak louder than words, as Mom always says. The Pitcher kicked Fernando's ass, paid Mom's doctor bills, and he coached me. I don't know much about marriage, but that seems like some good reasons to me.

So I'm like saying under my breath, *Say yes, say yes, say yes!*

The Pitcher leans forward on the bed, still holding her hands.

"Marry me, Maria," he says again. "I ain't a perfect man. You know that, but I will try and be a better man to you and your son."

Mom wipes her eyes again with mascara inking her cheeks. She stares at him. I see the trapped birds starting to fly and her chin starts bobbing. She is mad in her hospital bed and this makes me feel better. More like the old Mom.

"You think I need this? You think you have to *save* me?"

The Pitcher keeps his eyes on her.

"No, I don't. I know you don't. But I want to be with you," he says quietly. "I want to be with your son."

And Mom is staring at him, but the Pitcher doesn't move. He just stays in there like a batter not giving an inch. And then those birds in her eyes slow down and her chin stops. She breathes heavily. They are like that for a long moment. Mom looks up at him, then puts one hand on top of his, and touches his cheek.

She smiles.

"OK."

Now *that* is like a movie!

The nurse claps and Rev. Mike claps and I clap as Mom and the Pitcher kiss! And Mom, she starts crying all over again. Rev. Mike steps forward and the Pitcher stands up. I hug Mom and she's crying all over my neck and I get tangled up in her tubes, but I don't care, because she's happy, man. The nurses are fluttering around and the Pitcher and I hug. And Rev. Mike hugs *everyone*. Even the nurse is hugging and another nurse comes in, because I guess we need two witnesses for the ceremony!

After they say their "I do's" and kiss again, Mom wipes her eyes and frowns suddenly.

"Hey! Jack Langford!"

The Pitcher turns, this great big smile on his face.

"Yeah?"

Mom squints, her chin jutting out, eyes snapping.

"You didn't marry the illegal alien to get Ricky to the tryouts?"

The Pitcher and I look at each other as Mom holds up her iPhone.

"I got the e-mail yesterday from that crazy bitch."

The Pitcher shakes his head slowly and I look at him. I mean, that's not a bad play you know, but I don't think he rolls that way. It's like when I asked him in his garage the night before if he ever got lonely. I think the answer to Mom's question is in the silence, man. Because he never answered my question, he just stared at the game. But I knew then why he always had that television on.

"No," he answers, meeting her eyes. "I just don't want to live in a goddamn garage anymore."

Then he pauses and frowns, his face darkening.

"You didn't just say yes because you wanted your son to try out for the high school team?"

Mom leans back against her pillow.

"Hell yes!"

49

THE QUESTION IS, DID BABE Ruth call his home run against the Cubs? You either believe Babe Ruth called that home run or you believe he was gesturing. Check it out on YouTube. You see the Babe in the World Series, game three, standing there in Wrigley. New York is up by two games. They are tied with the Cubs four-to-four in the fourth. The Babe comes to bat and gets a couple strikes and let's a couple go by a two-two count. And then he just does it. He points to the centerfield bleachers and nails it.

Then he does that Babe Ruth jog around Wrigley Field.

So it comes down to what you believe about baseball, right? I think the Babe knew that somehow things would work out. If you think about all that's against you, then nobody will ever do anything. You just bet your dream will come true against all the odds. That's why I know the Babe saw that home run before he hit it. He saw it the way I saw myself pitching on the mound for the high school team. And that is where I am the day the scouts from college stop in the stands next to Mom and the Pitcher.

"He looks like a young Jack Langford," the one scout says with a cigar in his mouth.

The Pitcher shakes his head and spits in the dust.

"Nah. He's a lot better than that, rockhead."

And the scout stares at him and Mom says she isn't sure if she recognizes the Pitcher. He looks younger, if you can believe that. I think being married to Mom has taken years off of him. Mom drives him to the meetings where dudes stand up and say their name. The Pitcher has to say his name and admit he is an alcoholic. Mom says a couple guys didn't believe he is Jack Langford and he had to show them his driver's license.

The Pitcher set up the garage with a television and his La-Z-Boy chair after he sold his house. Shortstop now sleeps on our driveway. The Pitcher goes out there to watch his games and smoke, because Mom is not down with smoking since she quit. He even does some coaching with the high school and he occasionally uses a bucket of rocks. All the kids hate it of course. I have helped him a couple times and I had to show a kid more than once you can hit that knothole.

Sometimes.

The good news is Mom doesn't have to work again. The Pitcher put all his money in Coca Cola stock way back. I guess he's loaded. Mom never said that, but they went to Hawaii for a honeymoon. I went along. Pretty cool, bro. Palm trees and coconuts. I could dig living there. Mom only has one kidney now and has to keep her weight up. She has gained weight, because they do all those things married couples do ... like eating all the time.

Fernando split back to Chicago and I get Christmas cards from him and some woman who I guess he married. *Feliz Navidad from Fernando and Juanita* they always say. Hey, whatever. And me, I'm still pitching, man. I won't tell you where, but the Pitcher still coaches me and says I'm better than a lot of the rockheads they have pitching today.

The way I look at it is this: A long time ago I threw a ball under a garage where a retired World Series pitcher lived. And what came out of it was a change-up. In his twenty-five-year career as an MLB Pitcher, Jack Langford used a sinker, a fastball, a curve, and a slider. The truth is he never needed a change-up ... until he met my mom.

ACKNOWLEDGMENTS

Many thanks to Leticia Gomez, my agent, for persisting against all odds. Also to Joe Coccaro at Koehler Books for reading *The Pitcher* and seeing the vision, and for the very difficult task of editing. And thanks to John Koehler for publishing *The Pitcher* and bringing it to the world. And a special thanks to my son Clay for letting me hang around baseball fields and learn all about pitchers.

CPSIA information can be obtained at www.ICGtesting.com
Printed in the USA
BVOW07s1035060214

344148BV00005B/154/P